MARTINA C. BUND

WE CALL THIS LIVING

Novel

Bibliographic information
of the German National Library.
The German National Library lists this publication
in the German National Bibliography; detailed
bibliographic data are available on the Internet at
http://dnb.dnb.de

© 2020 Martina C. Bund
Manufacturing and publishing
BoD – Books on Demand, Norderstedt.

Coverdesign: Acrylic painting and foto
by Martina C. Bund
Translation in cooperation with Robert Hammond

First published by Oberbaum Verlag GbR 2008,
Berlin

Printed in Germany

ISBN: 978-3-751982863

For Ben

…an almost true story…

Many names in this book
have been changed to protect individuals.

CHAPTER I

Prologue

At the Bristol Hotel Kempinski Berlin I saw him for the first time. They had hired him as a bartender. Norbert with the blue crystal eyes, obviously Austrian landed gentry. I was in the first year of my apprenticeship. We still smoked and thought it was cool.

I fell in love. He did not.

Norbert always had another girl that was more his style. He found me great, because I drove a Karmann Ghia and had an apartment on the Fasanenstrasse, next to the Literaturhaus.

Every now and then I gave him a blowjob. It was so familiar.

After the wall fell, we drove to the East, slowly, a few metres at a time.

The Brandenburg Gate was closed to traffic; Trabi stench, unusual noises, mopeds with passenger seats, potholes.

It smelled different.

From Berlin-Mitte, Hoppegarten, Königswusterhausen to Potsdam. There were wide fields, hilly landscapes and lakes. On the way we wanted to picnic, driving along dirt roads, on and on the railway tracks, into the forest. We made love between ants and Greek yogurt and as proof that we were there, we tied my nylon stockings around a birch and laughed until we fell over.

It was a relaxing time. There was no Berlin Wall anymore.

We just drove on. At some point, when the evening came and the tank was nearly empty, we returned home.

Norbert had been disinherited by his father, because of Norbert's disregard for his homeland. He lived beyond his means and walked around in white pants and trench coat. But I liked him because he was different. People thought I looked like Joan Collins or Liz Taylor. Who has anything against that? I saw myself rather as a rebellious, though freckly, specimen of the new Modesty Blaise, who wanted to tear the world from its hinges. Brunette long hair well built.

How many times did Norbert come and ask for money, as I did from my grandmother. I paid, never expecting anything in return.

What I did not understand, was Norbert's special liking for drugs. He pretended to be a drug expert, but I did not take it that seriously at the time. I was natural, did not need drugs at all. I did not understand how drugs have gradually changed him.

Another Norbert lives in him now.

Feelings like concrete.

11 years later

There are days when your world suddenly changes.

I ate at Roberta's. Roast potatoes and salad and had a siesta in her guest room. She likes to rent it out to Berlin visitors to supplement her small pension. She is like a mum to me.

Roberta was a head nurse. She is more of an artist actually, composing and singing and possesses an Irish humour, matching her hair colour. She has a clarity that I have always missed in my parents' house.

I have to go to make a business presentation in an hour at the "Excelsior Hotel". Like every week. What should I tell people who have never heard of my business? It is Network Marketing. A business in the wellness and health area. It's about products that use natural energies to keep the body in balance. I work independently for a Japanese corporation that sells holistic wellness products worldwide through its distribution network called Vitessa. My task is to find people, who want to achieve greater physical well-being using these products, while at the same time, looking for business partners, wanting financial freedom from a self-determined life in network marketing. Can you understand that?

Network marketing has always been mysterious and adventurous to me.

Today there are other speakers. Luckily.

My thoughts are elsewhere.

Between my appointments I bought a pregnancy test, as I did before.

I spend my break at Roberta´s. When I see the result today, I feel like walking on clouds. "Melanie, you are old enough. Rejoice!" Roberta is right, with 34 you may have lived half of your entire life already. I turn and turn the stick; the result remains positive. Must go now. Cannot think about anything else.

The same evening, I bring the good news to Norbert.

He is against it.

"Remove it. A child is not a pet. Remove it!"

Mixed feelings.

I can hardly believe it.

Today I found out that we are having a baby.

I told Norbert. I was scared to do so.

He is totally against it.

I´m so sad.

In another financial situation, he might have reacted differently. He is so loving about his first son. I do not understand that.

What did I do businesswise? What did I sell? I have thirteen new customers with a turnover of around 10.000,- Deutsch Mark. Had not expected that I would have such a high turnover per customer. Every other day I have telephone conferences with my distributors.

For weeks after that, I was having an awful time. Norbert is always nagging me. He does not want it. He wants me to abort our child. No matter what he says, for me it is clear, I want my baby.

I want you to live.

The reason for my decision was probably the abortion in Greece.

I was twenty-one, in love with Costas.

The holiday flirtation turned serious.

We regularly commuted between Athens and Berlin.

My world consisted of this, educated Adonis and our future together, so I believed. His brother was always very direct with me: "You could be a star. With five kilos less!" How charming.

Costas, his brother and I had three stores in Chalkidiki, entrusted to us by his father as an investment for our future. A tavern, a supermarket, a disco. It went well. Seven days a week I did my best in our open-air disco by the sea. I organised the staff, the warehouse, and always mixed new cocktails. Our business was a hit. We made incredible money. With the sunrise, I brought the cash box to the neighbouring hotel, drove the staff home, and laid down for a few hours. When I got to bed, Costas had to get up. The rolls were delivered to the supermarket at seven o'clock. I became pregnant and wanted the baby. He did not. I needed to make sure.

We drove for an hour until we came to a supposed gynecologist. The practice was empty, more like an old apartment set up.

The rotund, elderly woman, posing as a doctor, was tall.

She spoke Greek and Russian. I did not understand either. Costas translated into English for me: "You are not pregnant. You only have an infection from the sea water. She will treat you!"

I trusted him, climbed onto the chair. She took iron bars and hot water.

No anesthetic. I remember my body shaking and the words "Poly ema, poly ema ..."

"Lots of blood, lots of blood ..."

The only thing she said, the only thing I understood.

Could not realise what was happening,

I did not know where my soul was.

Maybe it was with our child who just died.

After two weeks the cramps stopped.

I could fly home.

My Berlin doctor confirmed it.

Physically, I had got away with a tennis ball-sized cyst, but my soul had stopped breathing. My desire for a child was seared into me.

In what kind of world do we live?

Fifteen years have passed since Greece.
I experience the pregnancy pleasantly. I'm fine, no nausea or discomfort. Have baby things already. I'm looking for a name.

I worked with six wellness consultants from my team. Also, have given two presentations with colleagues in one month, had a weekend as the training assistant. And I always thought I was lazy.

The planned Volvo gives me cause to think. The sales management of Vitessa finances it only with my turnover. If there are differences, I must pay the rest.
I also have stress with Norbert.
The Sixt bill for his Austria weekend with the BMW has been debited from my account.

Preparing for the spring Expo. There are more new products, again. Tuesday wellness lecture, before that the management meeting. At the weekend I went with two new wellness consultants for an introduction to the preview, at the business centre Halensee. Slowly it gets too much for me.

Clinic Info evening in the hospital. I have decided. A water birth! Manon will do that too.

I'm mad at Norbert because he does not care.

Two friends have died of cancer.

At the best age.

S. leaves three small children.

D. had just become a father.

I get crazy about the idea that there is help, and the "people in charge" do not allow help. Through my business partners in Dresden, I learned about an insider article in the Swiss "Times Script", Phillip Day's unbelievable discoveries in his book "Cancer: Why We're Still Dying to Know the Truth". It has been proven that vitamin B17, found inside apricot kernels, sold in every health food store, can be lifesaving against cancer. If you have read that, you will have goose pimples. Am stunned how we are all treated as cannon-fodder. Cancer.

The truth never comes out.

In every third family there is a cancer case.

And in every family, as much as possible is done. However, the pharmaceutical industry calculates differently. Because of their financial omnipotence, millions of men, children, and women are not helped.

They let them die.

It was Bastian birthday today. My younger brother is now Twenty-six! We celebrate in his recording studio. Again, a lot of snow on the streets.

Norbert wants to help us now; we want to try it. Cooked together: Original Wiener schnitzel and salad.

For dessert we cuddle in bed.

I am straddling two horses at once, to be both, a businesswoman, and looking at my future responsibility as a mother. It does not seem so easy to do. Norbert still has no job. He is not a support.

I'm horny.

Mum and Dad bring a cot and baby stuff. What did I hear as a child?
"Maybug fly, your dad is at war.
The mother is in Pommerland, Pommerland has burnt down, maybug is flying! "
Maybe that's why the maybug disappeared from the scene for so long because they could not stand the songs of our parents and Grandparents anymore.

My baby belly is round and big. Today I gave my last presentation.
I'm sad.
Swimming was fantastic.

I float with my ball in the warm water and look forward to my child. Strange, so many big bellies, and yet everyone is left alone. Showers, creams, and everyone waddles back into her life.

The pharmaceutical industry is hot on the heels of the wellness industry. Anything else that could bring a breakthrough is picked apart.
Our drinking water quality is very questionable.

We tried to check the Berlin drinking water for drug residues.
No laboratory in Berlin wants to do it.

My little darling, you petal. You have turned! Lie with your head down, optimal position! Relive my body.

In the health food store, I discovered the magazine "Consciousness". The report on "climate collapse caused by weather manipulation" takes my breath away. It says:

"Did you know that:

- The sky above our heads has been sprayed since spring 2003 (possibly since 1999) with a mixture of barium salts and aluminum powder to manipulate the weather - and in Switzerland and Germany as well?
- These spray actions take place on an almost weekly basis across much of Europe, and are carried out by both the major airlines and NATO (Boeing) military transports?
- Censorship prevails in many media (press, radio, television) and authorities keep quiet about it? Some of them are trying to convince us that the tenacious cloud cover that forms due to the spraying is solely due to the increase in air traffic."

They are called "chemtrails."
In what kind of world will I see my child grow up?

Countdown

Appointment for flow measurement in the hospital.
Everything great.

For my baby!
Tobias, James, Jakob ... or whatever you will be called,
we both have nine weeks left to go. Never again will we
be so closely connected. You made it easy for me. I'm
curious who you are and what you look like. Have
everything prepared for you, and I wish us a nice birth.
I hope that you will always be well.
With love,
Your mum.

I have to take care of my new business partners, slowly but surely, otherwise the money will be turned off.
Can hardly sleep. My pelvis hurts.
The birth was probably my fault. I was over the appointed time. It was hot, the skin tensed. Unfortunately, I did not talk to the other mothers. Probably no one would have told me the truth. Code of Ethics?
This reminds me of the African circumcision that they call "ritual." Every day girls die.
Young women are mutilated forever, not just physically. I have read Waris Dirie's "Desert Flower".

After all, it will be my child

A homeopathy practitioner leaves me some globules to induce birth.
As soon as the beads touch my tongue, the contractions come with power. Stop! Can you undo this? Help! Breathe! Try to find a rhythm. Remember the birth preparation, how the midwife tormented us. I call Norbert.
He does not come until the evening.
In the car things are going through my head. I know the route by heart, telling him how to drive. I was alone at the antenatal class. It hurt to see how the other fathers were worried and looked after their wives.
After arriving in the hospital, I calm down, and get a room. Cannot sleep, always walking in a circle around the bed, until 5 o'clock. I am pushed into the delivery area. What about a water birth? After an hour they scare me out of the warm water. The contractions are so massive that they put me on a spinal cord PDA. No relief.
I survive on breathing and prayer.
Around me, women are screaming as if they were being slaughtered.
I despair and still smile like the Monalisa.
No scream, not a single one.
I breathe.
Norbert is there, but I do not feel it.
Have no one who really cares, no midwife, no doctor who encourages me.
I'm alone.

In the African bush this would be a death sentence. It is 29 hours. Finally, a doctor releases me.

Now I feel no more contractions. The tears are in my ears. Caesarean section. I am conscious as a team free our child. He cries. His head, bright red, pointed at the back, reminds me of a pharaoh.

They take him with them.

We give each other a peck. That's it.

Norbert hands me our son, he is healthy. Thank God! The baby is searching for my breast. Still have no milk. Ouch, it tickles!

We sleep well into the morning.

You have the energy of an angel.

What is your name? The baby says yes? Yes, Jakob. Congratulation cards, telegrams, bouquets and gifts are collected in our room. Norbert's roses let their heads droop the next day.

Three days later he throws me the documents for the naming into my food. I should deal with this by myself, downstairs in the hospital lobby.

"After all, it's your child."

Postnatal time

The day of our release from hospital was hot.
Norbert picked us up. Jakob is sleeping.
There are moments when the heart makes images
for eternity.

The postnatal time passes as though in slow
motion. Breastfeeding, sleeping, eating.
Every morning there are fresh rolls and
newspapers and in the middle of the breakfast
table, the baby lies in the baby seat, and we enjoy
all the different expressions on his face.
Norbert says he looks like Franz-Josef. The sunlight
is just too bright for him, hence the strong forehead
wrinkle. And with the birth mark he looks like
Gorbi.
Out of the blue, a baby acne appeared, so we could
only take pictures from behind him. Luckily, it did
not stay that way. The eye color changed from
paternal crystal blue to maternal chocolate brown.
Probably, nature has set it up like this: a week of
daddy color, so they'll recognise their offspring.
We even feel like we are in love again.

Summertime

Everything goes smoothly until the day I suddenly get knee pain. In the evening, I can hardly take care of the baby. The knee is swollen, hot and it hurts a lot.
Try to reach
Norbert in his apartment in Prenzlberg.
He comes late in the evening.
In the hospital, they puncture my left knee without anesthetic because I am breast-feeding. Torture.

Now I can finally scream. Only they cannot find anything and keep me there. With my baby. In our hurry we did not take anything with us. Norbert forgets us. I sink with shame.
After three days he finally comes, with a toothbrush and baby suits.
He has no time for us.
He has a visit from his holiday flirt.
They are making a pub-crawl.
On the Saturday after the visit, the nurse offers me a chance to be released.
At home, the fridge is empty.
All gone and used for his lady visitor. When I asked Norbert to bring out the rubbish, it came to a fight. He put on his shoes. I pleaded, begging him not to go now.
It did not help. He left without turning around.

It's the weekend, the shops are now closed, my parents away, Roberta too.

I still hop, my baby in my arms.
It is hot.
Berlin in August!
The radio is playing "Summertime".

Rescuing angels

My colleagues from *Vitessa* jump in.
Eighteen angels help according to the timetable:

Shopping, cooking, baby walking.

I am still suffering from severe pain and fears for
the future. When I look in the mirror, I do not
recognise myself. Sleep deprivation. Jakob wakes
up eight times every night.

The career woman who has always mastered all
situations confidently, where is she now?

I am getting scared.
Fear of responsibility, fear of the future.

My midwife tells me the truth.
She takes away illusions and hopes and speaks
plainly to me. Hammers me, like a dominatrix, but
now I know where I am.

I must put the whole bureaucracy stuff behind me:
education money, child support, maintenance.
What do I have to apply for and where?

I cannot make the move to social services yet. Have
the quiet hope that my independent business in
network marketing will recover.

Jakob, I want to protect you forever when I see you like this when you sleep. I have longed for you all my life and wished for nothing more than to hold you in my arms. I give you my strength, my courage, my days, and nights.

The conversion to the Euro has taken place, terrorist attacks on 11th September 2001 shake my basic trust. I am afraid.

Fixed expenses:

Expense	Amount in Euros
Rent	750
Childminder	92
Mobile	65
Land line	60
Gas	180
Food	350
Tax office	180
Electricity	40
Health Insurance	300
Hotel room rental	20
Minimum sales	200
Mailbox	45
Website	30
Insurance	120

Total 2.432,- €

Revenue:

Vitessa: 1.963,27 €
Child benefit: 150,00 €
Maintenance: 106,00 €

I'm missing about 200,- € in the wallet!
I cannot stand this for long.
Euro! That is twice as expensive!
Never before would I have paid 1.500,- DM for a 70m² two and a half-room apartment in Berlin Lichtenrade.
To this day I cannot understand why we do not demonstrate, boycott purchasing.
Why do we let this happen to us?

Operation knee

My knee: My orthopedist has not yet made a diagnosis until a doctor with a bare hand discovered a tumor. I will have to have surgery. There are in fact two tumors.

After that, Jakob sleeps in my arm. For a change, once a day, a nurse takes him out onto the corridor, walking and talking to him.

The past catches up with me

My dad sends me an SMS: "You have a longtime admirer, one with money!"
Should I convince myself regarding my father's recommendation? I fall off my chair in surprise when I hear the name. My former boss!
I had worked for the insurance company for six years.
For that gold digger and robber baron, I ruined my health.
From seven in the morning to ten at night, I was on duty for a higher intention. Every single hour I checked, with a new, different customer, the newly signed contracts from my eighty representatives.
If a cross was in the wrong place, I had to drive hundreds of miles again to have the customer countersign.
A telephone call would certainly have done it.
Sometimes I was bullied, even from other Wessis!
But because of that, I knew my way around East Berlin and the surrounding area well, drove across the German Democratic Republic and smoked like a chimney.
For me the end of the world was at the Polish border.
The massive potholes ruined one car after another, four cars from 1989 to 1995.

With the penultimate car, a white BMW, I invited the three children of a customer for a drive. It was in Angermünde. I saw them sitting side by side in the rearview mirror.

Very quiet.

No sound.

I just drove through the streets.

"Have you ever driven in a car?"

Shaking their heads.

"Only with the tractor."

The first time I visited, their dad opened the door in his undershirt. A small man who was hard to understand because some teeth were missing. I followed into the living room. They offered me one of the three chairs. There was a dining table and a TV which luckily was turned off. His wife was in a short-sleeved smock, rounder and taller than her husband. She brought me a cup of coffee, Turkish, and pulled out a small tin cashbox. Empty cans stood as decoration on a single shelf. A few football posters on the bare wall.

The children came out of their room full of curiosity. There were double beds, several. From the ceiling hung a rug that was supposed to divide the room in two.

The oldest boy had smoothed out plastic shopping bags and hung them up as pictures.

Sorrow welled up.

And then anger.

What do we mean by human dignity in Germany? What was I supposed to do here? Insure? Confirm the creditworthiness of the customer? Obtain confirmation from the employer that the customer is working and earning enough money?

The monthly contribution of his completed life insurance was 10 DM.

I approve the contract. At Easter and Christmas and in between I got postcards from these children. I never forgot that.

The father of a similar family from this place died shortly after the contract was signed.

I drove five thousand kilometers every month. Piles of signed contracts on my passenger seat, city, and road maps. On the back seat was "Zorro". My guard dog. When I drove home at night, I carried the entire day's collection in my suitcase. Long stretches of road went through the forest. I was scared when I had to stop around midnight in the middle of the forest at a railway gate. Not when my Rottweiler was in the back seat. I had become a workaholic. Norbert often took care of Zorro, especially when I went to Lüneburg or Zurich for seminars. The recruiting of the new distributors became more intense. Before the wall came down, we had once a month a seminar in Königslutter. Then every single weekend.

The final straw happened on Christmas Eve at 10.00pm, a distributor called to inquire about the tariff for dog owner liability insurance. Shortly afterwards I had my burnout.

As usual we were in Königslutter. Suddenly I could not move my head, my throat swelled, my eyelids became heavy. I left early, and somehow drove the two hundred and twenty kilometers to Berlin, went in the supermarket and shopped for a month and went straight to bed.

My entire gut was infected with herpes. My immune system had paralyzed me. Burnout!

I had missed the warning signals. Strange that one always takes the glowing warning signal on the car seriously but not for oneself.

Norbert walked Zorro, and went shopping for the whole six weeks.

The zest for life actually comes back when the doctor asks me a question: "Please calculate financing for a tenement block, we may make some business!" This triggers in my immune system something that brings me back on the path to healing. Good trick!

My career was at its zenith. An *Eppstein-Barr virus* in combination with herpes had triggered the *chronic fatigue syndrome*. An occupational disability was determined. Did I want that?

I decided against it and for a new beginning.

That meant a complete change in my way of life. Finally cook for yourself! Fresh vegetables, local fruits. Still water and herbal teas instead of coffee. No nicotine, little sugar. In the insurance agency, I got a separate office, which was sold to me as an award. The bullying goes on.

My burnout kicks me out.

I quit.

In the Holiday Inn, I hold my farewell speech in front of about two hundred colleagues, totally unprepared. After the buffet opened, the boss makes me jump into the cold water by telling me that I must announce my departure within a few minutes. I lost my appetite. Fortunately, I manage the speech from scratch. After five minutes everyone is standing, whistling, stamping, and for me it's time to leave.

We always have a choice

A crazy colleague gives me the idea to open a car rental company on Lanzarote. It won´t work, but I like the island. An island supposed to be made of nothing. Nothing but lava, I assumed.

Before I flew back, I got a job at the German radio station on Lanzarote. and within six weeks I sold or gave away everything I owned in Berlin.

I stayed for three years. I worked as a radio presenter, leased a restaurant in the seminar center for esotericism, opened a potato pancake bistro, which opened only on a Sunday, sold advertisements for a German magazine, sold cosmetics, gave riding lessons, sewing tailor-made clothes, worked in beautiful hotels, served in a tapas bar of a friend, and all that was not enough to live really well.

I was denied the announced severance pay from my insurance job, although I was entitled to two annual salaries. I had no legal protection, as my legal protection insurance was with the same company. If I had known that before, I would not have emigrated.

The only one who got a severance pay was the former boss and regional manager, whom my father now served up by SMS on a silver platter: Edgar Schrotz.

I think about it for a few weeks.

We always have a choice.

Jakob is not even half a year old. My professional and thus financial situation has come to a dead end. Life in sales has always irritated me, though it gives me enough recognition and variety. Financially, it is often a tightrope walk without a safety net.

We have good coaches. Every few weeks, events are needed to keep the energy up, and therefore the sales. I still try to visit the weekly presentations. The speakers I trained before the time of my burn out are now in the limelight.

Mixed feelings. On the one hand, I feel relief that I feel no longer needed, on the other hand only my child and a few consultants who occupy me on the phone really need me.

I catch myself as I feed my son on my left breast and send faxes with my free hand. I do not relax. I cannot enjoy these beautiful weeks of mother and child. The bills are a pain in the neck.

I do not get a dime from Norbert. Jakob needs hours to fall asleep. He hears every step. When I stand by his bed, I just want to look at him to recharge my batteries, I hardly dare to breathe. In no time he is awake and crying.

It's all about responsibility for my child. I did not expect that. I imagined life with my baby differently. I did not think of the real efforts and deprivations as a single mother. How long has it been since I went jogging in the morning, to the sauna or to the cinema in the evening?

Sleeping through. Time only for me.

I'm dreaming about it now.

Also I was very frightened.
Terrorist attack. Sept. 11th, 2001 in New York. Two fully occupied passenger aircraft fly into the Twin Towers.
U.S.A. takes revenge on Muslims and declares war on Afghanistan.
9-11 we will always remember you!

Over-excited

I'm calling Edgar Schrotz. He is on the phone and remembers my voice at once, even though seven years have passed. It all just bubbled out of me, I described my awful life situation, and asked him for help. I needed new salespeople whom I can teach network marketing to, and then get myself involved in their sales. Edgar Schrotz knows salespeople. The only question is whether he wants to help me, as a kind of referrer. I must tell him everything. I invite him to visit us.

I have the impression that he cannot follow me. I speak without a dot and comma, I'm probably over-excited.

We meet more often.

Unfortunately, he did not give me any recommendations.

However, he ordered the complete equipment of the wellness collection, worth several thousand Euros. I'm embarrassed, though I know that he can use all that for his health.

Another world

He buttered me up. I have the feeling of having solid support. When we want to love each other, it does not work. One day after it is better.
I believe he takes Viagara.
We see each other every day. From his house on the Havel he flies to Lichtenrade. He barely needs half an hour with his black Porsche. His fifteen-year-old son, Sasha, is often alone at night. Because of him I have a bad conscience. The ex-wife seems to rarely see their son.
Edgar can't be stopped.
I have a financial emergency. His is sexual.

It has become winter.
Jakob needs his child vaccinations. I have to miss his vaccinations. As a private patient, I do not have the money for it. I overcame my misgivings and asked Edgar if he would give me the money for it. He put three green notes on the table for me. I did not expect that.

New Year's Eve we are with his son in Grunewald, where I take notice for the first time of the clan of lawyers, pharmacists, and brokers. I have arrived in another world.
Feel the exclusion. They had declared Edgar crazy anyway. Because I'm thirty years younger than him. And then with a baby!

I could hardly afford my rent anymore. From month to month it was harder for me to make business appointments. In the spring we moved to his house. My furniture ended up at a junk dealer. Jakob is sleeping. His evening ritual is always the same.

Dinner, bath, creaming, brushing teeth, pyjamas, reading to him and music clock. I just hold his hand for a moment, let him fall asleep in peace. Have read a lot of guides. I find the parents' letters quite useful.

Secret phonecalls

Finally, after a long time, I can relax, enjoy the time with my child.
Edgar has a housekeeper, but there is still enough work left. Unfortunately, his adolescent son seems to be jealous of me. He hardly speaks a word. Maybe everything went too fast.

Edgar is sleeping. Frogs croak. The moon is reflected on the water. It's chaotic downstairs. Boxes, boxes, renovation, remodeling.
Everything will be fine.

I'm sitting in bed watching the lake through the giant window. Edgar's boat is in the dock and rocks in the sun.
But something is not right.

Edgar has not touched me for days. He makes secret phone calls, looks very thoughtful and does not seem to know what I am telling him.
He seems somehow absent. He says it's the divorce stress with his ex-wife.
A hug, a kiss would help me now. But Edgar can be so ignorant. He just does not see me. Even with Sasha he quarrels and roars around. I have never experienced him like that before. He also does not want to have anything to do with Jakob. I do not know what suddenly got into him.

The talk to his therapist seems to bear fruit. We were together last night. A sailing ship is passing by. It is warm but windy.

Turtles

We had a nice day. Have rested.
At 10.30 am late breakfast in the garden overlooking the water. Must pay more attention to my figure. Edgar too. We have discussed the subject of Norbert-Jakob visits. Not easy. In the afternoon we drove to Potsdam and watched a polo match. Jakob made his first steps on the lawn today.
The air smells like summer.

I have to earn money.
I never wanted to sell things and work in network marketing. And today I do both. Let's do something together as a couple. Why not? I need leaders in my downline. Do you remember?

Jakob is walking!

I don't feel 100% myself.
I have my period today.
Edgar and Sasha fly to Mallorca in three days. I'm looking forward to this peaceful time. I want to change basic things with me. I have to organise myself differently. I miss my books and concerts in the Philharmonic.

Edgar is in Mallorca and enjoys the peace. He is probably looking for rare turtles, which he can smuggle with his suitcase into Berlin. Sasha is with him and will probably be bored with the turtle hunt.

The first days I missed him, but now it is alright.
Jakob and I have time for each other, have fun.
The private zoo is regularly fed.

Jakob could not sleep. There is a lot going on in his mind. Maybe because he saw Norbert. We met at the playground.
Norbert said that if he had loved me, he would not have left me.

Edgar and Sasha are back home.
The holiday has done them good.

Fog everywhere.
In the bedroom, the wall is mouldy.
It disgusts me to see that.
I put my mattress in front of Jakob's bed.
The craftsmen have to prise open the whole wall.

Tonight, Edgar came to Jakob's room where I slept on the floor. He wanted sex.
I pushed him out the door and then locked up. He probably had drunk too much or had been watching porn.
It disgusts me now when he tries to kiss me. He has bad teeth although he could afford the most expensive ones. He smells like an old, sweaty, lonely man.

Rich in experience

I despair, I do not know what to do anymore.
He wants to blackmail me. Edgar took the car keys and pram from me.
He wants to force me to sign a private loan agreement for a sum of over thirty thousand Euros. I did not get this loan! Of course, you have done something for us, bought me clothes in the department store. There are three pants, two jackets and two pairs of shoes. I needed them urgently. The things from before my pregnancy have not fitted for a long time. My friends gave me sweaters. I already feel like a beggar.
You also gave me something for Jakob. I was able to get the essentials for him at H & M. But even here I was thrifty. Often, I go to the secondhand shop. But you, Edgar, even put the party on your list, and Jakob's dining chair, I do not understand.

Panic!
I cried, I fled in despair with Jakob and the baby carriage to our favorite park.
Called Edgar's daughter in law. "Now calm down. I will tell Jürgen and he will come by." Try to relax. How do I get out of this situation?

Edgar seems to be hot-tempered, throwing things around, with a bright-red face and gray, raggedy hair. Even fully packed boxes down the stairs. He yelled at me; he wanted his money back.
He did not stop.

His oldest son Jürgen has arrived. Mumbling as among men who speak the same language, only because they are father and son.

Jürgen once told me he would not even go to the old man's funeral. How crazy is this family?

They both drive me into a corner.

I have signed.

Edgar had already set up a loan agreement, with interest. Everything is completely insane.

He wants thirty thousand Euros from me.

Why did I ever trust Edgar?

The only thing we take with us when we leave this Earth is experience. So, I will be rich when I die. Rich in experiences.

Torches in the snow

We have got a flat. In Potsdam, directly above the horse stable.

The move went well. Except for the interruptions of Edgar. At the loading dock, he had the relocation helpers open every box. He had found nothing of his precious belongings except for a small bedside lamp.

I organised everything myself. I am finally free again!
To celebrate the day, I am with Jakob, in a restaurant, high up on the radio tower of the Berliner Funkturm.
An unforgettable experience for us both.

I am so glad that we have now found a good childminder.

If Jakob annoys me by fiddling about with, sockets, stove, fireplace, PC, or machines of all kinds, I blow my top.
I cannot really relax right now.
My office will be ready soon and I hope I will be successful there. I can give demonstrations.

I'm proud of my own wellness studio. It is located directly at the entrance of the riding hall. The paddock from a stallion is only a few steps away. I hear him neighing.

We have mice. Today I saw one run up one of my briefcases.

Hopefully, the landlord can come up with something. This is probably the reason why almost all apartments are empty.

I am a bit confused. Had a meeting with Edgar today.

He told me he has breast cancer. He had known this since the summer and did not say a word to me. His cancer has turned out to be benign, he will survive everything.

That explains a lot. It upsets me. So many retrospectives, puzzle pieces which now give a fuller picture.

Despite everything, he must accept that things are now better for me.

There is no way back. I wish you a wife that suits you and makes you happy.

Just before Christmas. My boss is celebrating her 65th birthday at the *Café am Neuen See*. Torches in the snow, along the red carpet to the entrance. Hundreds of candles and fairy lights. Enchanting! Finest floral arrangements, fireworks over the frozen lake, selected dishes, and nice guests.

I dance barefoot.

Moments of happiness.

Jakob is already sleeping with his childminder.

Happy New Year!

Jakob has the measles, as we learned today from the pediatrician. He slept early on. I hoovered the apartment very quietly, scrubbed the closet doors, put in the washing, and watched television. The Christmas tree is still standing. At midnight Ute Lemper came on TV and sang: "What a Wonderful World".

Norbert wished us light and love, by SMS. He always does that since he has started visiting the Tantra men's group. From Edgar a call with New Year's wishes.

How I wish I could get rid of him.

Everything too gray for a New Year's Eve.

The trap is snapped.

The mouse is dead.

One is still alive though.

I sold my first wellness package today. Although at the purchase price, but I'm glad about my first sale in the new year.

While bathing, I put Jakob's back in my hands. His hair floated around his head and he sang.

Damn it. Edgar wormed his way around me again. Do we have a chance? I wish that he would finally dress more modern - a younger partner would then be more appropriate.

I'm tired. Jakob was at the osteopath's today.

"Knackfußindianer" he calls him.

The osteopath has been able to regulate many problems which were caused at the birth. The whole treatment cost me sixty Euros. By the way, there is now an awful war between U.S.A. and Iraq. Peace hopefully should prevail.

My body is small in relation to the soul.

The complex with an equine clinic and all the trimmings, makes a great impression on me.
From the two rooms, we can watch the blacksmith at work. It smokes, then stinks of burned horn. Quaint.

Bills pile up

Speakers Training:
Sylvia has introduced herself too late and does not respond to the different communication types, does not come across as businesslike.
A little more neutrality would be good.
Newer, more enthusiastic junior speakers come into action.

Edgar was here today.
He gave me some lingerie. All very posh! I had a bath. The foam smelled of jasmine, the water steamed.
I tried to relax. I did not try to think about yesterday and tomorrow.
I have a bad conscience.
Feel like I have been abused.

Meeting in Stuttgart.
Our economic situation in the country currently means:
A longer growth phase comes to an end. Fourteen million unemployed. Old and young. Pension situation. Health situation. Two-tier society. A problem cannot be solved by the mind from which it was created. More trade without intermediate trade. Barter: cosmetics for software. Flexibility, the courage to change is in demand. Become part of the future!

The bills still pile up. There are more, more, more. I do not know how to deal with it.
I let my anger about me and my financial plight out on my child.
It is not Jakob´s fault, he is only a child. Too often, I exhort him. "Do not do that, get away from there, stop, stop that." I often complain loudly. I hate myself for that.
Now I am the way I never wanted to be.

I want to leave it all behind.
Jakob builds a stage out of a wooden box, takes the toy he got from the circus as a guitar and sings like a star. I am amazed at his repertoire. We sing, read and paint together.

Edgar does not irritate me anymore.
Our chemistry is not right. We never matched anyway.

I look forward to the walks with Jakob.
We are collectors, we pick meadow bouquets, find stones, bark, feathers, dried snakes, dead moles (cat`s leavings) and accumulate them as souvenirs on our staircase.
Rediscover myself with my child.

Although Norbert comes irregularly, but at least once a month, Jakob should be able to build a relationship with his dad.
I hope Norbert never brings him into contact with drugs. Then I will become a wild animal.

Edgar is not leaving me alone. He comes to me almost every day. But his alleged love does not seem to be so great that he would destroy the extorted loan agreement.

I must get information from a lawyer.

Boppard on the Rhine, great work with the downline. The constant ups and downs in sales! Are all these twists and turns really healthy?

Hope remains

People come and go ... who stays with me?
What is left for me?
Moments: music, a few tunes.
Hope remains - and courage.

I read a newspaper: "The World", an Editorial.
"The rich get richer, the poor poorer"
by Ulrich Clauss
Creating the split
"It may be lamented, ideologically charged or simply ignored - the facts themselves remain indisputable: the gap between "poor" and "rich" is opening up ever wider in our society. Whether one attaches this to disproportionately increased manager salaries, to stagnant or de facto sinking real wages, to disintegration phenomena in the social systems, to the labour market, to education or to media consumption the finding is always the same. The growing material and life-world division of society is a fact.

In politics and social science, a lifelong lie has stubbornly survived, which is owed to the social state-antitotalitarian founding consensus of this republic. It is the heresy of the "leveled middle class society".

From the press: "Work and capital income are developing in an exponentially increasing extent. The social security systems are increasingly financed by the relatively declining wage share and must be reduced accordingly. The political parties - from the Greens to the CSU - respond to it to this day with simple self-deception. In the pension, social health, and infrastructure sectors, too, the reversal of what has been and still is a stated policy goal can be observed.

As action again makes better insight into incapacity for action in the long term, the consequences are as follows: The statistically contaminated equality promise of our political system cannot be upheld because nobody can and will pay for it. How much energy will be released if we finally say goodbye to the unattainable goals of our failed social-state philosophy? "

I had a "family constellation according to Hellinger". Clearing the energy of my ancestors and in my immediate family. Do I have my own?

CHAPTER II

Above the clouds

Jakob sleeps in the window seat, his cuddly horse in his arms. I look at his small hands, his breath is even. Stewardesses have looked after us. Children around us are impatient and tired. Last time I was on Lanzarote I was with Norbert. There was constant bickering. The last one was because he constantly had to smoke next to me and I was already pregnant. Now we are alone. I'm really ready for a vacation. We are pale, we have bleary eyes, we do not look like an advert for the wellness business. I spontaneously booked the trip on Saturday, a last-minute offer.

Famara Beach. Looking up from the beach to the steep coast. It fascinates me. For years, this scenery hung in my living room, photo after photo, giving the whole panoramic view. Fond memories are revived.
My island.

Katharina was my best friend on Lanzarote. I wish she was doing the Vitessa business alongside me. We would then have a business base here as well. That would be great!

The best part of Christmas

Edgar picked us up from Berlin Tegel airport. I did not want him to do that. The plane was late. He just wants to confuse me all the time.

How annoying! I must find a man who is totally there for me, who loves me and with whom I can be really myself.

In one of the songs from Abba, they sing:

"Try once more, like you did before."

I will! Be sure, I will.

Christmas. Jakob comes into the house, rosy, red cheeks, a Christmas elf.

The elf hat dangles over his face, so he can hardly see. At the childminder's, he made and painted things for me.

"Here you are, mum!" Jakob looks so cute.

This is the best part of Christmas.

I hardly have any money left. I'm at the end of my tether.

I found the solution!

We move to Lanzarote.

I want to start a new life.

Maybe I have better opportunities to do business there. I can certainly use my contacts from the past. I will try it. We will stay there for six weeks and see how it goes.

I already have a plan: Sabrina, the daughter of Siegrid comes with us as a babysitter. I phoned her yesterday. We already know each other. She has a semester break, from studying law in Dresden. A nice girl has a sense of responsibility and can get along well with Jakob. She takes her books with her. We live in the house of Kruse. They have given us a fair price. We pay 20,- € per day. Car hire and food will cost more. Adventure! Hopefully, it will bring a perspective.

On 24th February we depart for Lanzarote.

The finances worry me the most. I do not want to let Jakob know about it.

Probation

Find no peace in the siesta.
Saturday afternoon, the birds are singing, my thoughts, my emotions are bubbling. Vitessa on Lanzarote becomes reality. Let's see what happens to Christa. And maybe with Katharina. Will you be my business partners? They speak fluent Spanish. I do need them.

The way to the future lies ahead of me.
Sun, sea, colors.
I'm so thankful.
Gracias.

The internet does not work, neither does the DVD player. After all, the first wellness consultant starter package for Lanzarote was delivered yesterday, all the documents in Spanish.
Today comes Katharina, can't wait!
I am sitting in the shadow of the palm tree. The wind brings sand from Africa. The day is young.

The *Stern-TV* showed late yesterday a broadcast about the people in Afghanistan. The women want to sacrifice their children for the so-called holy war. They are prepared with breast milk for the war.

Sit alone on the beach of Playa Quemada.
Playa Quemada means "scorched earth".

A special place. Dropouts and hippies live in small old fincas along the coast, there is only one row. Otherwise only campo, and two old bodegas, which are still exactly as before. It was the last place I visited before I returned to Berlin six years ago.
The waves tell me what I do not understand yet.
What happens at night in the sea?
Only a few people know.

Wind, hair dangling, shivering.
Look into the infinity.
The Channeling has advised me that for my future I should start writing. The evening is coming. My Vitessa vest is awesome, it warms and protects me, I love it.
I will meet Katharina in Tias.
I have questions about the school for Jakob in the future.
I came here in the tapas bar, where I was ten years ago. Nothing has changed here.
Luckily.
The only new things are the CD player and the ice chest. Who is dancing with me?

Cesar Manrique

For lunch we were at the golf course restaurant.
I met Henri, formerly of restaurant Ikaro. Great pleasure! He says he thinks of me every winter; his old oven was mine. The best thing is that he has offered me a house in Tahiche, for 750,-€ per month, with a pool. Do not want to get too excited. He is going to call me.
Cannot believe that.

The wind gets stronger.
Last night with Katharina in Tias, all my business cards flew off in all directions. While trying to catch the cards we had to laugh so much that we almost wet our pants.

Today we were exploring the island. La Santa, a training center for top athletes, with gigantic waves on the doorstep. For surfers and windsurfers, it's a paradise. Then we drove via Mozaga to my former employer, the *Finca Florida*. It looked dead. Only the good old housekeeper was still there. With the serenity of a goatherd he told me everything.
They have no more horses.
I remember riding Carlito to Famara.
On the endless beach we went racing.
Only once was I second. Before heading home, we would relax a bit in the tapas bar while the horses had some water. Scenes like in the Wild West.
Once upon a time.

Our tour continued through the volcanic mountains Timanfaya, where I always feel sick.
The lava below the surface glows, the energy is too strong for me.
On the black beach, Playa de Janubio, we spent an hour collecting the bright green Olivine, semi-precious stones in all different sizes.
Got a good complexion. Jakob too.

Today I got Henri's confirmation for a house with a pool. I'm so happy!

My dear Jakob, now our new reality begins! A new life. You are still so small; you will be three years old in three months. Of course, it is not easy to have me as a mother. But we chose each other.

Today the owner called me and canceled my house again. I'm not getting upset. There are cosmic laws that are going their own ways. Jakob is much more likely to upset me. He constantly unhappy and moans, nags and gives no rest.
I'm probably just too concerned with the financial worries and trying to build my business here, that I do not really notice Jakob enough.
Claudia in Berlin told me that it must have been similar in my parents' house. I always just went along but was never seriously respected or asked for my opinion.

Today we look at an apartment in Puerto del Carmen. Yesterday I quit our apartment back home on the horse farm near Potsdam by fax.

As for Christa`s and my cooperation, I'm really confused. I thought she would want to change her life. Something is blocking her.

We are about to leave for home.

The six-week test living abroad was worthwhile. The response was great. Above all, I found an exceptionally good customer and recommender: R. She has influence and a good reputation and will be a useful contact for me.

It seems that the wellness idea is so popular, much more than I expected. We had over twenty-five appointments with a turnover of over two thousand Euros per week.

Nevertheless, Christa does not want to do the business. Cannot understand that. Still need to find someone who can translate my lectures on health and wellness for me into Spanish.

I do feel surreal.

Life forces me to make a decision.

A book by Cesar Manrique helps me. So, I decide: I plan to come here in late June with all our belongings!

My little darling, I hope you will like it too. I hope all goes ok for us. My old new home. Lanzarote is like a mother. No matter how I am, no matter what I do, she loves me.

There I have more peace in me.

I drink the water like wine.
Should we go to "Puerto del Carmen", the tourist capital, the Waldorf kinder garden or British private school? I must decide. It is getting serious.

We found a Waldorf kinder garden. Rochelia is called the children's lady. Her hair goes down over her backside, black and shiny.
She pronounced your name: "Jakob", with a deep, Spanish timbre. Then she spoke to you in Spanish, and you answered in German. You had forgotten your horse. The next day it was back. The French little girl, a neighbour, has found it.
"It laid on the stones!"
The nursery house was built from bits of wood that a man had collected from all over the island. The main entrance is surrounded by a magnificent Bougainvillea, like a canopy of flowers in bright pink.
In the garden chickens are running with their chicks.

Relief! Tomorrow at 5pm we get the lease, from Julie in Puerto del Carmen, Calle Alfonso.

One step to the next.
Silence.

Back to the future

Finally, we arrived in Potsdam. Jakob cried at the door, wanting to be "Back on Lanzarote!" The tension fell away from him. Now also from me. Mum&dad picked us up at Tegel airport.
"Were you not afraid?"
"Nah, mum held my hand.
Look, I have very dirty hands! "

Four days ago, we were still there. Seems to me, like an eternity. Now we are back here, with my parents, and my granny Klara.
In Potsdam, on the estate, everything is as usual.
Jakob had his first day with the childminder again, she surprised him with an Easter party. Egg hunting in the garden with the other kids:
hot, cold, warm ...

End of June we fly.

Stress.
Lawyer´s appointment draws a blank.
All deadlines for opposition have expired!
No solution in sight yet.
Our flights are booked.
One-way.

Jakob stays with Grandma and Grandpa today.
He looks forward to it.

They rarely take him. Even Grandparents who do not have a single parent daughter take their grandchildren more often.

Afternoon appointment with Edgar at the playground.

Hope for a solution.

Mother's day

Jakob: "Horse, we move to Lanzarote, but there's no bath just a shower. But there is a big sea with very high waves!"
Horse asks: "Are we going there by car?"
"No, we're flying with a plane. Do you know what our plane is called? Yes, do you know that? Our plane is called Air Berlin. Exactly, they will fly us there."

A bouquet of red roses is on the doorstep. With a letter. It is an Invitation for a meal with asparagus. Edgar picks us up.

Dark clouds loom. It forebodes rainy weather. Jakob watches the weather house closely.
"I have asked Edgar a question and told him something as well. I told him that we were moving to Lanzarote. Then I asked him if we could take the car on the ship. Edgar said yes!"

"What did you do Jakob?"

"Yes, Edgar said yes. Yes mum!"

The car was seized shortly after Jakob's third birthday.

Leadership meeting Hannover. On the way back home an accident happens, at one hundred kilometers per hour. A woman drives into us.

I'm sitting on the back seat. At that moment I do not notice anything unusual. The very next day, my left arm is numb right all the way down into my hand. Must have massage treatments regularly. It turns out that there are three herniated discs between the third and seventh cervical vertebrae. The insurance companies cannot agree between themselves.
It hurts so bad.

Edgar has indeed installed a listening device in my apartment. I find it in one of the files that are next to the telephone! Who would do a thing like that? This is going too far.
I called the police.
The charge is against a person unknown.
Though I know it was you, Edgar.
Do not understand why.
Sabrina did not pass her university examination in Dresden. This is not a lucky day!

Raisin cake and cocoa

Lounge with a red stole on the sofa. I'm empty. I have no strength. Paralyzed.

Yesterday it happened. We were at home.

On the neighbouring property there is a white tent, in front of an organ grinder. Nostalgia. Jakob and I are standing in the door listening as if he's just playing for us.

The phone rings:

Morales from Lanzarote. I do not understand everything, she talks so very angrily and too quick. Excuse me, won´t we be able to move into our apartment?

I cannot believe it. I tell her that a friend will contact her.

I try to contact Roswitha.

She does not call back until the next morning. She has spoken with Morales. In fact, the deposit check could not be cashed. And now? I have already packed.

It is five o'clock in the morning. Potsdam. Pigeons coo. Drinking yoghurt with barley grass juice, I am looking good. I am awake.

At last Roswitha calls again. She is a sweetheart.

She could get us a bungalow near her, costs a bit more, but has a swimming pool. Everything has its good points.

My left arm hurts.

Waiting for the injury compensation. Today I hold a presentation in the retirement home in Pankow.

The chief secretary of Vitessa called me:
My salary! All gone to Edgar Schrotz!
In my naivety, I have missed all the time limits of the forced loan.
Now he is also officially in the right.
Half of each bonus check should go to him.
He wants to totally destroy me.

My days only consist of packing, giving away and throwing away. I have sent eight packages by mail. It seems endless.

In between it was Jakob's third birthday. His half-brother Elias (as it is said, but a brother is always a brother, right?) came too. With his mum.
We understand each other okay.
The furniture was already gone. On the stairs we prepared a picnic overlooking the fields and the neighbouring farm. There was raisin cake and cocoa. While we took them to the bus, I pushed both boys on the bike. The large wooden locomotive of Jakob was in tow. We gave it to his brother as a keepsake.
We waved until the bus disappeared.
It's night. I scrubbed like crazy. My hands are rough. There are fourteen pieces of luggage. I registered the excess baggage on my "Air Berlin Silvercard", it did not cost as much as expected. We're sleeping on the floor this last night,

on a mat. Unusually hard. Hopefully everything will work out with the taxi and the airport. Manon will be there.

Adventure

I have a whole flock of guardian angels with me. Manon has everything under control. She hypnotized the gentleman on the Air Berlin counter. After some too-ing and fro-ing everything worked, except for two suitcases. Incredible. Twelve pieces of luggage without a cent excess baggage.

Then we were called on the airport tannoy, urgently:

"Please come to security immediately!"

The batteries were still in the torch. Safety regulations!

With the big cuddly bear under my arm we climbed onto the plane, the last two. The move had begun.

After five hours of sleep, we landed in our new home, Lanzarote.

The sea sparkles more than usual.

It smells like adventure.

Jakob holds onto me tightly. Friends are awaiting us, with their bright, tanned "Welcome!" We distribute the cases on three cars. My red bike has a flat tyre, and Roswitha with the bungalow key is not there! I reach her by mobile phone.

"Melanie, something terrible has happened, you must come immediately."

Just arrived, my knees wobble: our new home has evaporated yet again. Roswitha has completely fallen out with the Canarian landlord.
There was no turning back!

Jakob sings and dances and splashes in a green plastic bowl.
For two weeks we can stay in one of Roswitha's apartments on the Costa Teguise.

The windsurfing World Cup is taking place under our very noses. Insiders would envy us.
I enjoy the colors of their sails, how agile and fast they are. Here I am sitting in a deck chair and just look at the sea.
I cannot unpack the suitcases.
First, I have to find a real apartment.

The move cost me all my strength. Dad has had to lend me five thousand Euros, mum will count that against me forever.

Norbert does not care about us.
Edgar did not want to let us fly.
We had to take extra support at the airport, leaving Berlin, against Edgar.

Tias

We finally stay in Tias. Next to Katharina. A semi-detached house with two bedrooms. Her Swiss neighbours have let us have it for three months. Everything is so new and clean.

However, when we moved in yesterday, Jakob painted with his crayons on the steps, meaning "we are here now and stay here!".

The familiarisation in the kindergarden is difficult for him. With his childminder, there were only three. Now there are about twenty children. There are four Maestras, Rochelia is his favourite. I was with him for a few hours. Now I have to work and earn money. It must happen somehow. What shall I do?

Jakob reminds me that in Potsdam we were often with the horses: "They wanted to eat so many carrots!"

I plan to open a small wellness hotel. It is called the *Finca Ernandez*. Three double and four single rooms, each with bathroom, a dining room with sea views and three sun terraces. The lower floor should remain private. There is a heated pool.

The property has almost six thousand square meters, only it is above the golf course, unfortunately it is not next to the beach.

Actually, it's not too expensive, but I still have to find a way to buy it. Hope for Roswitha's commitment as equity partner. She is already a successful businesswoman with her own apartments and will be able to assess the risk.

When the bank manager approved my financing concept for the *Finca Ernandez*, my soul reacted with migraine.

I have never had migraines. The heat wave with forty-three degrees Celsius only adds to my distress. It actually gets too hot for me.

I refuse the bank´s offer with a heavy heart.

The coffee machine is awesome, a typical Swiss make. Everything in the house is new and beautiful. The only disadvantage is that, in three months, they want to use their house themselves, so I'm allowed to unpack only the bare essentials again. It's frustrating. Otherwise it is fantastic.

The duplex is next to Katharina's. We do not talk over the garden fence; we go straight round. The doors are open anyway. Katharina reminds me a bit of Marilyn Monroe. She even has the beauty spot is in the same place. She is beautiful, has a good sense of humour and is enterprising. I wonder why we never got the right man. Less talented are obviously luckier. Katharina has a crush on a full-bearded Cuban. Not my type. She melts like butter in the sun. And they make music! Yesterday it was, an impromptu rehearsal at Katharina´s. The whole band was there, all from Cuba, making music as if they all played with the same heartbeat.

All babysitters have surrendered.

Screaming attacks without end. The director of the Waldorf kindergarden called me. Could I please pick up my son? She could no longer take the responsibility for Jakob. Otherwise, he may become traumatised. What can I do?

On the same day, even more happened. Jakob distributed a litre bottle of suntan oil over the living room floor until it was empty. Jakob was proud of it and was happy! When I finally had cleaned it all up, I could lie still for a moment, grateful that the, brand-new, cream-colored fabric sofas had not gotten a drop.

As I lie still, I hear some strange noise. Sound of water. Water? Water! Jakob?! A waterfall runs down the stairs. Jakob had discovered the bidet; he was trying to make a fountain. I put him on the bed giving him instructions to stay there. At the same time, I throw blankets, towels, and rugs onto the mass of water. As in a trance, I repeat my mantra: "That cannot be true. That cannot be true!"

Luckily, there was no slap.

My warning bells ring all the louder.

Fruits and sparkling wine

They are there! Claudia, Manon and Loni. They booked an apartment from R. and got our very first place.

As a greeting, I have provided a platter of fruits and sparkling wine, perfect for the first view over the sea.

It's night. Read Claudia's manuscript. I am encouraged that I can do that too.

Loni and Jakob understand each other like an old married couple.

Betunia gave me a massage. The left arm hurts.

I sent the insurance company a fax. Have yet to write to the Federal Supervisory Office and also to the accident insurance.

Claudia really knows her way around children. In Berlin, she set up the children's help-line call centre. She reached Jakob's inner self through his cuddly horse. Finally, he starts to open up.

Manon reads and writes a lot and thus relaxes, away from everyday Berlin life.

The beach is right in front of the house. A dream. They all look so well-tanned, much more than we do.

Picked up Janine from Arrecife airport. She will be our au pair for the next five weeks. She is doing an internship to improve her Spanish, that the *Waldorf* kindergarden arranged for her.

She is beautiful.

Half Eurasian, slim, with almond eyes and long dark hair. It seems to be going well with Jakob. I am so relieved. Everything runs well. I'm surprised how Janine copes with Jakob. Today she even ironed our laundry, and all of that by herself.
With Jakob she shows an almost an angelic patience.
Janine has fallen from heaven. A gift!

Our friends from Berlin have already left.

The Big Bang

Today is Janine's flight back home. I'm so sad. Jakob too. We will miss her so badly.

A massive bang, then others. Don't understand what has happened. I am in shock.
A young Spaniard hit us with his big BMW this banged us into the taxi in front. The taxi came back from the front and hit us, which in turn forced us into the BMW. We perceive impatient horns, police, and ambulance sirens. Big row in the middle of the old town, in a one-way street. Fortunately, there are witnesses who prevent the gentlemen from simply driving away. The paramedics open my door.
"Como tu llamas?".
Jakob is calm. Apparently, nothing happened to him. Thank God. He was buckled up. Jakob sees how the men in white first examine me, and then put me in the ambulance. General Hospital. Emergency. At first it is very quick. Wheelchair, cervical collar. Then we wait hour after hour. Others seem to be worse.
Every now and then we get a cup of water.
We are released at midnight with X-rays and a cervical collar.
The next day Katharina picks us up with her car, shows us where our car is parked. It is still roadworthy. We drive to the beach, to the best ice cream parlour in Puerto del Carmen.
Jakob gets his lemon ice cream.

I take a café con leche.
Five days have passed since the accident.
Jakob told his little horse everything. Again, and again.

Quiet.
The sun gives me something comforting.
Diamonds glitter on the infinite blue Atlantic.

My shoulder, left arm, and hand are partially numb. My neck hurts the most. The examinations have shown that I have three herniated discs. The insurance company does not accept the diagnosis as an accident. They think it is a sign of wear. There is at least a little compensation for the pain and suffering, of 820 Euros
Feel worn out.

ATM

A special day. Something new starts today: I can rent one of the massage rooms in the seminar center if required!
Walter and Heidemarie will soon come from Switzerland and will want to go live in their own house, which they have kindly rented out to us.

Through friends we found an apartment in Los Molinos. The swimming pool is huge, in the middle of a botanical garden. House-high rubber trees, palm trees, Aloe Vera, blooming cacti, bright bougainvilleas, occupy gardeners full time. The pool area has a lifeguard and a "sheriff" with a pointing stick.
We get our mail twice a week from a Senora in the office. In addition to bills and Edgar's nasty attorney letters, we're happy to have a few lines with a ten Euro note from my Grandma. Sometimes even post from mum&dad comes with a photo or admonishing newspaper articles.
I'm wearing a black swimsuit and shorts. Jakob has his striped baseball cap on. In the children's pool, he dares to jump off the edge. At first shy, then he is unstoppable.
Our evening meal consisting of toast with cheese and Guyayabe tastes excellent. So, we get over the fact that we can't afford ham or any other luxury at the moment.

I am at the ATM outside the Hotel Playa Roca. The insurance company dealing with the first accident has transferred the money.

Jakob waits ten meters away in the car. When I get back in, Jakob sees the banknotes in my hand, and I see how much it affects him.

Jakob wipes away his tears silently.

I had no idea how my child felt our needs.

This moment burns in my soul.

In Germany, the chocolate Santa Clauses will probably be on the shelves now.

Here, it's always summer.

Thirty-eight. Sometimes I feel old, all chewed up.

On the other hand, I feel like a child that never grows up. What am I not growing out of?

How do my parents do it? Do they even worry? I blame myself for this situation.

Now I am sitting with my child on Lanzarote and have no fixed income. I only have sixty-five cents in my wallet. There are two litres of milk, three eggs, potatoes, and toast in the fridge. I have baked bread in the freezer, its rock hard. I consider putting the bread in water and try to bake it again because it would be a shame to waste the flour.

November 2004

Hello mum, Hi dad,
just come from the massage studio. I am glad that the therapy actually helps. The sun is shining, hopefully also with you. The sea sparkles 250 m in front of me. There are two cruise ships in the harbour. I am considering how I can sell my wellness products to those tourists. By the way, the bank kept my card at the machine because of the tax office and blocked it. It is not possible to withdraw anything from the German account. I will send you my Spanish bank details again. It is very urgent!!!

My greatest gift to you would be if I could invite you to stay here with us in "Los Molinos". You would like it. You could certainly paint pictures out on the terrace. It is spacious and has sea views and shade from noon onwards. Jakob and I are going through a phase of defiance. No matter what I do, say or ask, I always get a "No" as an answer. Dressing, brushing your teeth, creaming, eating, drinking, etc., always just "no". It is not easy. Come to my limits, then we both cry and get along again.

Now an exercise for you against aging if you want: try to tell each other how it was before you met. From the way to school, the classroom, what was the name of the teacher? What was going on during the holidays? What was your favourite thing to wear? Favourite Food? Birthday reminders? It trains the brain and I realise that at the age of 38, I have a little trouble remembering and telling Jakob all about myself. See you soon, sending you some Canarian sun and regards, Your daughter

Get up. The thermometer shows 26 ° Celsius at night at 2:39 am Canarian time.

I get some fresh air. Jakob has crawled into my bed. He sounds sniffly. Today he can give me more comfort than vice versa.

I cried. I rarely read the tabloid press.

How I, as a good mother, put my own interests last, at least I talk myself into it, so I read in bed after work until my eyes start closing. For me, reading is a luxury. Now I was satisfied with the election results, and also read the interview with ex-Chancellor Schmidt and admire not only his wrinkle-free (worry-free) skin, but also his ideas for the federal budget. The fact that I am not alone with my debts does not really comfort me. But what got me out of bed and shocked me so much? Page 3. The horror gallery: 13 murderers who raped a 5-year-old boy to death. Germany this summer. An incredible reality.

Why is that happening in Germany?

Is that one of the reasons I'm on the run, one of the reasons, why I don´t like my home country?

Lanzarote didn't ask me anything, just let me be. Weeks have passed. I am realising more and more that it really is that I am creating my own reality.

When I insert Mozart, I listen to music that I've always loved. It is like meeting a friend who sings and dances with me, who knows my soul to the very last corner. A friend who is always loyal to me and with whom I can rely on totally. Is there such a person?

Music.

Who the hell has decided that the news must only report such terrible things?

Does it help me? Does it let me grow, does it let me feel my potential?

Am I forced to buy the newspaper? Am I forced to turn on the radio?

Am I being forced to turn on the TV?

Do the media want to toughen us up?

Who can stand all this?

Why don't we fight back?

We arrived here in Lanzarote a few months ago, me and my three-year-old son. No full bank account, no rich lover, no wealthy Grandma. But of course, a family and friends who are with us in our thoughts. Only I can help myself. I listen to heartbeat of life. What is my lesson today? Would my life be more exciting with a thick financial cushion? Ver unlikely. But that is my belief, that I want to change. Hey, how exciting would it be to help another person with money? Now I want to help myself first.

The `schoolmaster of finance` warns:

"Pay yourself first!" I feel like being in the TV show *Generation Game*! I need a toaster, TV, vacation trip, car, dishes, pots ...

I never want to have to sell anything to anyone anymore.

I should go through the country like a wandering preacher, "Take and buy or leave it!" I don't want that anymore.

The straw that broke the camel's back was a gentleman, who did not show up for his massage today, nor did he cancel. But I still had to pay the room rent, for nothing. Enough.

"Okay, I'll give you some paper and a pen, then you can start right away!" Was Jakob's answer to my declaration of intent to write books now. Sit in front of the radio and think about the old days. The Beatles, Elvis, Abba, Barbara Streisand. I dive into a world. Sometimes I understand how autistic people must feel. Stevie Wonder, Barry White, Stephanie Mills, Sticks, Earth Wind & Fire, Diana Ross, Michael Jackson, Bee Gees, Madonna, Queen, Whitney Huston, Kate Bush, The Carpenters, Eartha Kitt, Joe Cocker, George Benson, Sting, Elton John, Chris de Burgh, John Travolta & Olivia Newton John, Cool & The Gang, Grönemeyer ...and many other great musicians.
Thank you all!

I'm happy to have a real girlfriend.
Katharina lent me some money.
Hope we will be better off soon.

Ten more minutes, then close I Ronny's shop for designer clothes. Glad that I can help out here and there. It's fun and I need the money. Unfortunately, it cannot be with a permanent contract. In the

beginning Jakob didn't tolerate a babysitter, then they hired Christa, to replace me. Understandable but it´s a pity!
I must pick up Jakob from the kindergarden and then return the rental car in the afternoon. I just see a woman attaching notes to palm trees. Must I have to do something like that? Am I right here?
I cannot enjoy my island.

Betunia and her partner were there. They want to work with me. Everything in Spanish! What a strain! What fun! Just explaining the word `aim`, by using the idea of a marathon run, gave reason for much laughter. Betunia speaks English to me, they speak Spanish to each other, I think in German, try to express myself in Spanish and add in English. Chaos or art?

Los Molinos

Grandpa Albert has died. He had a full life. Lived anew every day. With gratitude. Grandpa Albert was so modern, he knew what was good for him and what wasn't. He treated everyone with respect, including me. He had turned ninety-four.

Wrote to mum&dad.

Hello you two!
We hope you are well; I believe it was extremely tiring in Braunschweig for you both. We are doing reasonably well, except for the financial problems. It gives me a big headache and I urgently need to increase my income. Jakob now has friends in the Waldorf kindergarden, he is in love with a 2½ year old girl. The weather and nature are fantastic!
Greetings to you
   Melanie and Jakob

At eight in the morning we come to the parking lot. A tiny black kitten sits and meows in front of "our" car. The little kitten just fits in my hand. All way over to the kindergarden, Jakob is completely thrilled by the cat. Must focus on the traffic. On the way back I get cat food and a worming treatment. We call her "Peacy".

Katharina found a shop in Arrecife, opposite the jobcenter office.

There she will offer her service to women for the "Make more of yourself", style advice and make-up courses for people of all kinds. Additionally, her artist agency for musicians is going well. She is out and about even during the evenings. Carlos is on his own, but he is thirteen years old and he is very used to be on his own. Nevertheless, Katharina is a loving mother.

She offered me a chance to use her shop for the "Vitessa wellness concept". Although I love Katharina like a sister, I am skeptical.

A big mistake

It is a time when I feel so lost and can no longer find my way. I miss the regular "parent letters" (www.ane.de) from Berlin. Jakob challenges me. My strength is running out.

It was bad yesterday. I put Jakob under the cold shower three times! I don't know what to do any more.

I made mistakes; I must learn from them. I am solely responsible for my child. Norbert does not answer, does not answer the phone, doesn't answer the mail. I cannot cope with his irresponsibility and ignorance. I need a lawyer to claim maintenance. The German youth welfare office paid me 106 Euros per month until I left, which is so very little. Now the child benefit is no longer applicable. I was unable to pay the rent for the first time ever.
We have to get out of the apartment in ten days.

La Gomar

For how much longer can this go on? Depression. I feel better when the sun is shining, or Jakob is in a good mood. The positive thing is, that Walter has offered to rent me the car again.

I decided to buy whole grain bread instead of stamps for the last 1,80 €.
The photo shoot for Katharina's new image catalogue went well! She is a professional.
One day of manicure, four hours with the hairdressing team, three days in boutiques until everything matches and the accessories fit. The lady, who was supposed to create beautiful eyebrows for me, was so quick and careless, that the treatment gave me two black eyes and a week waiting for the swelling to subside.
We only need two hours for all the photographs. The photographer praised me, asked me, if I was working as a professional model. The panorama of La Gomar already looked like the Blue Lagoon. I was allowed to keep most of the clothes, and the jewellery. The photos are great.

Christmas Eve is in three days. Santa Claus brings my child Lego bricks and gingerbread. For me a kimono that I discovered for 20 € in an Asian shop. I received further rejections of my job applications. From the airport and the health food store. There are almost no jobs without shift work. On the other hand, I have a new customer for Vitessa. It is the boss of the *Restaurante Estrella* in Yaiza, Mrs. Fürstenberg. Her house is classy, stylish, and creative. With antique furniture and a pool instead of a patio.

On the second day of the Christmas holidays, I see the pictures of the tsunami disaster, pictures I cannot believe. I am scared.

We moved out of Los Molinos on the day before New Year's Eve. Katharina found us two rooms in an apartment in Arrecife. Alisa and Bibi are friends of Katharina. It is the first corner house directly on the beach road, near the *Grand Hotel*. I pay a third of my previous rent. A fair price for the *Edificio El Islote*.

Liz gave me Pinky's number. Pinky was one of the first German settlers on Lanzarote. She was the wife of a well-known industrialist who cheated on her with his secretary. She knows the VIPs of this world. Pinky would bake waffles for us, smothered with guyayabe jam. We have loved her ever since. She celebrated New Year's Eve with us in the *Hotel Teguise Playa*. There was a glamorous show with all the magic, decorations, and funny costumes. Just the thing!
Jakob got two apple spritzers, I got two Campari and oranges.
At twelve o'clock everything sank into a fireworks frenzy. "Happy New Year!"

Los Reyes

From the winter garden you have a view over the ocean. I see the volcanic chain of Puerto del Carmen. There are four bedrooms. We were able to rent two. I set up my office in one. The room we sleep in faces the laundry room. The salon is as big as all the bedrooms together. We often eat together in the kitchen. The pantry is well stocked. Everyone has their own shelf. We have tested Alisa's Christmas chocolates. They melt on the tongue and smell like almonds. She has got so many of them. Alisa has her own bathroom. She does slave labour for a real estate shark. She needs the money. Her mother owns one of the largest estate agencies in Madrid. But at some point, she wants to work for herself. She can do it! Small but powerful! Her hair is as black as that of an Egyptian, her dark eyes are even more striking due to the deep, black eyeliner. Alisa exudes "joie de vivre", I was missing that. Bibi is the quieter one, although she is three years younger. They both like to laugh, especially because of the muchachos. Bibi is still a trainee in a property manager's office. She spends her lunch breaks in the car. It's not worth driving home, she says.

Unfortunately, our flat-share friends all smoke. But they only smoke when the window from the winter garden is open. Peacy jumps easily from one window box to the next, we are on the third floor!

The corridor between the salon and the front door is so long, that Jakob uses it as a racetrack for his wooden scooter. The cat always chases after him. Our friends like to come and visit us.

It's almost a bit like the time when I was living in Lichtenrade, and my Vitessa team came visit me almost every day. We sometimes go down to the sea after dinner. When the sea is rough the spray splashes on our faces.

Pinky tries to get me a job in the *Hotel Beatrix*. In vain. My Spanish is too poor.

We want to witness the parade of the three Kings on January 6th from Pinky's balcony. first row! We drive towards Puerto del Carmen until Walter's Corsa´s engine fails.

With the last swing I head up the hill to Tias and let the car roll on to a parking space. That's it. At the same time, "Los Reyes" turn their camels around the corner, surrounded by a crowd. Mostly children.

We got there at the right moment.

So-called luck amidst misfortune!

It rains sweets, the children screech. The parade gathers in front of the stage under bright spotlights. From the loudspeaker, a deafening Christmas speech by the mayor. The Kings dismount from their camels. The turbans glow white, with gold-trimmings in their precious robes. On the stage they take a seat on the thronelike armchairs and give each child a handful of candy, one after the other, with great solemnity.

Jakob doesn't want to, too many people, and it's too loud. I understand. We go over to one of the pavilions, where hot cocoa and donuts are served. Next to it, are the bodyguards, police with flashing lights. One beckons Jakob to sit on his motorcycle. My little darling is embarrassed but is still happy about the tempting possibility for days.

Pinky is waiting for us in vain as our car has broken down. By foot it only takes a few minutes to get to Katharina's house. She drives us to Arrecife.

Tomorrow she wants to tell W. about our mishap with his car. How embarrassing.

I had put off the oil change. That was the reason for the engine failure.

Of course, I have to pay my share, I promised. How shall I pay? Wait for compensation. Every week I get massage, electricity and Fango. Nothing really helps. The repair is still pending.

From the flat I can always see the same guy as he assigns free parking spots to drivers and gets tipped. When does he actually sleep?

Two thousand Euros I have to give back to Katharina. From that money I had bought the TV, the DVD player, and an electric heater. With the rest, I was finally able to settle my other debts and fill the fridge properly.

Jakob has finally settled into his kindergarden. The rituals give him security.

He sings the Canarian songs in a chanting, sing-song voice. I only understand half of it, but it means a lot to me watching him. He turns the songs into a stage play with recurring themes. His lady in the kindergarden thinks that Jakob speaks fluent, accent-free Spanish.

A decision

Dearest Grandma,
Today I received your life-saving letter. I thank you from
the bottom of my heart! I think you can feel how I am,
how we are. You were also a single parent for some years,
just like me, you fought for yourself and your child to
have your daily bread…

I wonder why I often have so many difficulties.
Why can't everything go well for a longer period of
time?
I can decide what I think, I can decide what I feel.
Who dares to tell me how I should be, how I am
allowed to live?
During childhood, our parents tell us
what we should do,
in school, the teacher tells us
what we should do,
when learning a job, the mentor tells us
what we should do,
then the banker tells us
what we should do,
the partner,
the TV,
the adverts,
the press,
the bailiff,
what I should do,
what I must do.
Do I live my life or do others choose for me?

We are blocked off, not listened to, not accepted, excluded.

"The greatest evil we can do to our fellow human beings is not to hate them, but to be indifferent to them. That is absolute inhumanity."

George Bernard Shaw

The time has come for changes.

What I bought today:
1 toast, 8 yoghurts, apple juice, 1 tin of cat food,
1 kilo of rice, 2 liters of milk,
1 small salami,
1 kg of sugar, 2 oranges,
1 cucumber, 3 apples, 2 donuts.

Total: 16,86 €

Grandma had sent me 20 €, so I had 3,14 € left.
I still had 80 cents, ten potatoes and some frozen cake.

Decided.
We leave.

It took me a long time to find out that I would rather live in Germany than here.
Nature is fantastic, the climate is wonderful. Palm trees, sandy beaches, sun, light, brightness, flowers, and the music of the guitars. I will miss that. I will not experience the Canarian fiestas in Germany either. Maybe I will have something else instead:
My family, my mother tongue, writing, art, old friends, and hopefully more financial security.
I sit in chaos, all around suitcases, bags, boxes, dust. Farewell. It shakes me, can only cry, feel a sense of loss.

My decision is made. We're going back to Germany. There are also doubts. I ask myself if I am not going insane. Sea views, temperatures around 25 ° C, palm trees. The simple, but hard life. Hope I don't make a mistake. Still, something is missing.

Jakob tells himself something in Spanish. I spoke to Rochelia, the kindergarden teacher. She was telling me about Jakob, that his constant kind of masturbations were not so normal after all. 'It is becoming an obsession'. There are two hearts in his chest. A very gentle one and one that is uncontrolled. She also says that he speaks Spanish perfectly.
"Sin accento!" Even now that I'm listening to him. Increible! "Los angelitos..."
Rochelia thinks that it takes two years to shape, to help him develop... "cuidar". She is sad that we are leaving.

Playa de Reducto

Jakob builds a sandcastle. Wind blows, the sun will soon set. Construction site noise behind us. Jackhammers, circular saws, trucks unloading. The workers come from Cuba, Colombia, Argentina.
They think about their wages, about their wives, about their children. And then?
Then comes the reassurance and stoicism from the result of their inner plus-minus lists. And that's called resignation at some point. In between there are also siestas and fiestas, the pain is bearable. And they can make music!
Viva Cuba!

What was on my lips

It's 1.30 am. Today I worked as a waitress in a bodega in Tias. At first it went quite well, there was even a tip.
But at some point, it struck me as strange.
"El chefe" was messing around with his bartender and was really cocky. Then I saw an inhalation device behind the counter. The two were taking cocaine.
Shortly before midnight I went to take a sip of water.
An almost invisible gel was smeared on my glass, right on the edge. Disgusting, slippery, sour.
My circulation goes down immediately. It makes my mouth dry. I feel dizzy. I'm in the bathroom, have to spit. I feel an unknown pressure in my side. Help!
The alarm sirens ring out inside me. Alarm!
Policia!
Okay, okay, keep calm, imagine nothing happened. I spat it out.
I can only wipe away what was on my lips and in my mouth, I can't do more now.
Stop drinking water, stop drinking here, never again!
I have to calm down somehow, not show anything. Keep going. I desperately need the 40 Euros. That damned money! Didn't say a word. I pulled myself together. Now I really know what it means to pull yourself together.

I gave the babysitter 10 Euros.
Babysitter Eva, a close friend of Bibi and Alisa, had come over and brought her lover with her. Alisa is in Madrid. Bibi is with a friend in the cinema. If only I had not needed the money! I wanted to have a police raid on the bar, with blood tests and everything that goes with it. Who allowed you to abuse me?

Alisa has quit her job. Congratulations! Would like to learn from her how to sell real estate and to teach her network marketing in exchange. If I knew it all. Tomorrow I can fill the fridge and thepetrol tank. Finally.
We will be home in three weeks.

Peacy

It rained. For days. Jakob writes a letter to his father on the PC We have had no sign of life from him for many months.
The very old fashioned computer's paper clip cartoon rolls her eyes and smiles mildly.
Jakob allegedly has chickenpox again.
I have the shingles.

We are having breakfast now, with Waldorf meadow flowers from Rochelia on the table, candlelight, and salsa. Where did she find the flowers? The day after tomorrow, we're off to Berlin.

Mail from my mum. In the envelope 15 Euros.

Jackhammers and heavy machinery continue to work. Building dust and noise whirl up. The windows in my little office room are so dirty that I can only imagine the house opposite. When I wake up today, Peacy is on my chest. I can't stop some silent tears. The cat puts a paw on my mouth as if to say:
"I know, you don't have to say anything." Now she is sleeping on my lap.

A night without worries.

- 6.24 am: Get up before the alarm clock rings
- 9.30 am: Marianne is coming to help us.
- 9.45 am: Maja arrives with her bus
- 10.30 am: With scooter, bike, child seat, pram, we have in total twenty pieces of luggage. Someone in overalls is right outside the door, tinkering with his car. An unexpected angel! He helps with the mountain of luggage and even drives some of it to the airport. I am so grateful!

- 11.30 am: Airport.

There are two hundred and eighty-six kilos. I only pay excess baggage for a hundred. There are four Euros per kg. Dad must help me please. Where can I find him? Mum&dad are not available. Leave a message on the mailbox. The credit card no. was noted on the ticket reservation, so the excess baggage can be booked. Dad calls back, encourages me. Five minutes later, dad sends doubts by sending a text message to my mobile, whether everything is correct. Can't change anything now.

- 1.00 pm: My first café con leche.

For Jakob, a raisin roll and apple juice.

- 2:00 pm: Grit is coming.

We can't take three suitcases they are just too heavy. Fish out some of Jakob´s picture books, my X-rays, and our Easter decorations from one of the suitcases that Grit will kindly take with her. Books, files, and evening gowns stay here.

- 3:00 pm: Boarding at last. The hand luggage is heavy, too heavy for my intervertebral discs.
- 4:25 pm: Delay due to snow in Berlin.
- 5:00 pm: We sit in the aircraft, rolling towards the runway. The machine stops after five hundred metres. We have to wait. Go back.

Nobody knows what's going on.

Jakob is very patient, but finally wants to see his grandparents. We sweat in the glazed hall.

They try to repair the on-board computer all afternoon. Without success.

"We ask the passengers booked to Berlin to go to gate No.21!" There are chips with schnitzel and salad. Think of Norbert's schnitzel.

Once upon a time.

- 8 pm. Everyone must get their luggage, we too. The powerful pair of electricians help me. Angel in action again!
- 9.30 pm: Arrival by bus to the marina in a new five-star hotel. Jakob and I run the bath water with a lot of foam. It is the most beautiful marble bathroom I have ever seen. I am grateful to spend a night in luxury. As if fate had made up our farewell.

A night without worries. Buenas noches.

C H A P T E R III

Berlin

We have been living for three weeks in my old children's room at my parents. I can bear it. Jakob too.

His Grandpa patiently plays with him and his new crane. Circus variations are the latest hit. New figures dangle and balance, clowns hang on the trapeze. Nobody is allowed to enter the room, that's a man's world.

It is cold. Two degrees.

The cherry trees have grown up. The bird feeder attracts some heralds of spring. Jakob is supposed to be in the Waldorf kindergarden in Zehlendorf. Let's see. Otherwise I am quite confident. I have a 400-Euro job with a company car in the dental laboratory in Potsdam.

You are not forcing me into the life that you have intended for me. The Job Centre wants to wear me down so that I take on any job, no matter what.

I would love to work, so please give me a job. Every week I apply again. Single parent with a small child, I am not even invited to interviews.

I've never been unemployed before. It is the first time in almost twenty years.

I would love to work, believe me.

Got twenty-two awards and certificates, but it doesn't really help.

Berlin!

There you are again, you old diva. Your thousand faces you show me, dazzling, plebeian, also in your finest outfit. Do they also have a brain? The Berlin air with a Grunewald fragrance. Are you from Klein-machnow?

You old circus horse, whether you don´t work at all or perfectly, just like clockwork. Berlin, you make me crazy, what should I do with you?

Here all seems to be right, here all seems to be important, but on the other hand nothing really matters. Berlin, what a little darling you are.

Nobody can be harmed by you.

You are and remain Berlin.

And my sweet darling sleeps like an angel with his cuddly horse and dog. Yesterday he wanted to put his Grandparents into prison in his rage: "There you can think a little about the rubbish that you are chattering and so mom and me could have the allotment garden just for us, right? And besides, I still have two other grannies! "

And how will it be in a hundred years? Different, dear gentlemen! And whoever is not able to understand, whoever does not go with the flow, will disappear. That´s the way it is. So, flow with the change of time, be there before her, be always one step in front. Don´t you know, you must have arrived before you have set off, said old Jonathan seagull. But how on earth do you do that, without flapping your wings? So, do you really believe, that you will arrive, if you will not set off?

Jakob is out of breath, pausing his bed hopping. "If you hop too, the pain of your arm will melt away!"

Too many questions

Pope John Paul II dies tonight.

Conversation with god. Do I love suffering so much that I am closer to God? God, you wanted me, like every other child on earth.

I sorted out bedding with my Grandma. She has twenty-five sets of bed linen, we only three. Have the impression that I just pack and unpack.
Finally taking root, is that possible?
Wannsee. Deliberately I hang up notices in this area. I want to give my child and me security and some standard of living if that can be planned at all. Wannsee. How long do you want to give us a home? Hopefully, everything works.
Logical that the apartment is not forever. It is small but inexpensive and is paid for by the Job Centre. In the next six months I want to register my business again and earn some real money.

Puzzle pieces

The kindergarden is special. The children are free to move around, to invent games themselves. The educators are Manuel, Sandra, Barbara, and Marie-Carmen.

Marie-Carmen is Mexican, so Jakob can continue to speak his Spanish. What a coincidence, but anyway I no longer believe in coincidences, only in puzzle pieces that gradually form a picture.

We get basic security, the child benefit is of course there, maintenance too. The rent should be taken over by the Job Centre. We can have two rooms. So, including the rental costs, I get around 950 € per month.

I'm so happy that Jakob gets an organic lunch and lots of fruit in the kindergarden.

Three candles

I went to the church in Ludwigkirchplatz, in the middle of the week. Wanted to pray.

A homeless person distracted me. I walked through the central aisle and just opened another Bible.

"You are only in a hurry and have appointments, but you are probably not taking the essential time, time for love. Love is the essence of life. "

Three candles were burning.

Sit at the Job Centre. Are there any jobs here? Now the clerk will want to interview me first.

Jakob splashes in the garden with his water slide, which he got for his birthday. Now a new phase of life begins. Yesterday I attended the last Vitessa presentation. It feels like a lull.

My kidneys hurt. I must be careful with my health. Indian Summer. It was raining heavily yesterday. The air smells fresh and clear, like on a Sunday.

I just watched TV, *Inside these four walls*. I was really moved, how the children and mother cried out of happiness for their new apartment. I need something like that too. Just someone who is generous to me and Jakob, helps us to feel better.

I am just beginning to realise how grateful I am to Roberta. She visits Jakob once or twice a week. She goes with him to the Stölpchensee. Or to the "fairytale forest", where she always invents new stories.

Norbert never calls. If he feels like it, he calls up out of the blue and then we must have time for him immediately. The other way around, he never has time for us when we need him. Especially when Jakob writes to him or calls him. He simply doesn't call back. Jakob feels that his father is not reliable. It is so little that we want. The youth welfare office pays me Jakob's maintenance, so I can avoid that discussion with Norbert.

Still in debt and other pain

I receive:

       785,00 € from the Job Centre including rent
+   127,00 € maintenance from the youth welfare office
+   154,00 € child benefit from the Family fund
=   1.066,00 € per month for a two-person household.

From which I pay:

      395,00 € rent
      38,00 € kindergarden
      5,00 € parental contribution day care
      150,00 € food
      65,00 € telephone with flat rate
      35,00 € mobile phone
      60,00 € petrol (15,00 € per week)
      40,00 € electricity
      50,00 € water and additional heating costs
      60,00 € pension insurance
      46,00 € credit card payment
      62,00 € car insurance
      21,00 € accident insurance

=   <u>1.027,00 € total sum for outgoings</u>

I have 39,00 € for extras like birthdays or hairdressing.
If Jakob is interested in learning an instrument, I will save the money elsewhere. Education is important. The ID for the city library costs ten Euros a year. This works out okay. What I really miss are concerts or going to the cinema. It's hard

to believe that my standard of living has deteriorated so rapidly.

I don't give up yet.

Dear God, make me debt free.

Caring for our landlords´ garden is fun. Jakob enjoys the raspberries. It is nice to see how my child feels about flowers and plants.

He speaks to them. When we come out of the garden, we are always better than before.

Jakob came to my bed around six o'clock today.

"Mom, please promise me that there are no bad people in the morning, only in the evening, yes!?"

I tell him that there are no bad people with us anyway. In addition, he should always remember that his guardian angels take care of him.

"And the good God too!"

"Yes, Jakob, of course."

That seemed to have calmed him down a bit. I covered us. He was with me, very warm. Then I noticed Jakob trembling. Since I have already registered that he masturbates without shyness, I assume it would be that time again. I turn around with my back to him and exhort him to stop. I can't go back to sleep like this. After a few minutes I notice that his shaking is not getting any less, and I assume that he would continue. Then I understand that his hands are not under the covers, rather that Jakob is trembling with fear! My goodness, my little child, what is he afraid of?

The next day, Jakob is waiting at the window for his dad.
Norbert arrives finally.
The atmosphere is already full of aggression.
I'm on the phone to Claudia, we are discussing the arrangements for her gala, almost in despair.
I should never have offered to write up the minutes from a meeting for her, as she was struggling to get everything ready for the gala.

Jakob and Norbert are in the forest, with their bicycles.
His email afterward his visit was pointless, disrespectful.
Why?
Must he always want to hurt me?
I do need to draw a stronger line between us.

Certainties

Yesterday I started to dispose of the first photos that held me back. It is good to get rid of your past. On Sunday, Omi tells me that she can't understand, why, my mother always kept putting sugar and honey on my dummy.

The dentist at the time in Wilmersdorf, then told her off:

He had never seen children's teeth like this before! There was a black line across my milk teeth. I was fed too often, almost stuffed, and then crammed in nylon clothes. Why did you treat me like that, mum? What I needed from you, was just love, acknowledgement, encouragement. The feeling that you are proud of me, as a mother. I did everything to try and please you, to hear from you that I am good at something, anything.

I am your child.

Jakob, sleeps at Roberta´s. She ordered me to rest in bed. Roberta conjured up potato pancakes with apple sauce and real chicken soup!
I should better sleep. My lungs are heaving, trouble to breathe, my immune system is weakened.
Our only certainties are the kindergarden, sports, Sesame Street, Roberta and Grandma Klara.
Everything else is out of reach.

Sunday morning, 8:34 am I opened the blinds a little to let the day in. Fresh air after the rain. Got my menstruation. Well, we know the program, it all comes at once. I guess it will remind me to rest. The way of the old, former life has slowly come to a halt.
Is the new life already waiting? With curiosity and a little impatience, I want to peek around the corner. Read T.C. Boyle, Albert Einstein, Fengshui, a book on creative writing and Hermann Hesse. Poems by Erich Fried. Again, all at once.
The first early cars splash in the puddles. The rainwater flowing down the slope is already rippling like a small stream. It sounds so comforting, and yet it flows fast, you could almost sail small toy ships on it.
"Pride and Prejudice" Jane Austen. Been to the cinema with Elke, first time for a long time. Feel like a teenager. Everything is possible.
Who loves me? Which man is to be my husband?
My polar bear is loyal to me, it warms my backside.

Poverty in Germany

I finally want to be the woman I really am. Deep down, my soul trembles with longing for liberation. How do I take the next step? I always run away from myself. Hide away, afraid to fail. Frustration and pessimism want to creep into my thoughts. Help! Fortunately, it is already 1.46 pm in the afternoon, my alibi for a siesta, that I got used to on Lanzarote. I long for security and love and I am ashamed of it. I can't always be strong.
Dear God, send some new people into my life.

Berlin newspaper. Front page:

**"Child care agencies raise the alarm:
2.6 million (2.600.000) children live in poverty. "**

According to the German Child Protection Association (DKSB), far more children and adolescents live in poverty in Germany than officially stated. DKSB President Heinz Hilgers spoke in Berlin yesterday of 2.6 million minors. That is scandalous.

Hilgers requested significantly more help from the federal government for poor children than previously planned. The child supplement for low earners must be increased from the current 140 to 175 Euros per month. From the third child onwards, it should be 225 Euros. Hilgers said that in March alone, 1.929 million children under the age of 15 lived in families that depend on unemployment benefit. Older children were not even mentioned in this debate. Information from the social assistance and asylum seeker statistics would have to be added. Hilgers believes that politicians must think that the number of boys and girls in poverty will increase despite the falling unemployment rate.

This morning we woke up before the alarm went. It is still dark. The windows are steamed up like every morning. Did it snow again? Familiar sounds of garbage collection.

Everything still sounds like it is soundproofed, even though the snow has already turned to slush. Seems to be slippy. My car is probably the only one in town that doesn't have winter tyres on it yet. I'm thinking of yesterday's shopping, which I managed to do with my last 5 Euro note: oatmeal, milk, a bottle of vinegar to clean and 12 free-range organic eggs. Keeping free-range chickens has been officially banned for bird flu for months, hasn't it? *This chicken lays your egg!*, was the cover story once, showed a sick, plucked animal at eye level. Out of sight out of mind.

So, I'm driving to the secondhand winter tyre warehouse in Spandau. I use the traffic light break to wipe the fogged windows. Still see everything blurry. Again, why is this a phenomenon that apparently only affects me? The cars to my right and left all have a clear view. Probably a "Freudian" topic. Clear view of my life, have I ever had it?

Classic radio manages to help me escape my reality for a few moments.
Mozart.
The twenty-first.
My music!
On a small cloud of timeless happiness, I travel to the most beautiful memories and into the distance to my prince, who is already waiting for my first

119

kiss somewhere. Where are you? Do you think of me even though we haven't met yet?
When will I meet you?

Still so icy. Minus twenty degrees Celsius. Fortunately, we have it nice and warm. We feel comfortable here. Jakob says the only thing that bothers him is the cemetery across the road. When we moved in, we went for a walk to get to know our new neighbours. Apparently, that's what I told the cemetery gardener. He then showed us the grave of the *Iron Gustav*.
I believe with such revolutionary neighbours, that's right!

Something new really starts today!
The contract for my distance learning has been signed. I'm so happy!

I read in the edition of the German Red Cross:

Definitions, when are you poor?
Who is considered poor and who is rich - that depends
on the society in which someone lives...
In 2005, the poverty line in Germany was 938 Euros.
Other definitions of poverty emphasise that income is
not the only factor. In the life situation concept, for
example, poverty is associated with an undersupply in
various areas of life, for example in housing, health,
work, and education.
One thing is common to almost all definitions:
Those who are poor have less chance to fulfil themselves
in the society.... "

Watched a nice old movie on MDR. Romy Schneider and Alain Delon in the leading roles. As a couple in a large villa with a pool somewhere in France. I adored her. Her looks and manner were more than charming. I liked her voice best. It sounded so special.

Omi said for the first time today that it will probably be "her turn" soon.

How am I supposed to survive this?

You told us stories about hamsters and air raid sirens and how you cheated and made your own `cracked eggs´. Another story was the one with Grandpa's hat and the fat farmer who was supposed to give you some ham for it. You put the hat on him, and you almost peed in your pants with laughter over his puzzled face. Then there was the story of the stolen cement, smoke in the parlor from the tiled stove, Hetti Mikkus the laughing pigeon, and your own mum, who never spoke about her parents.

Omi, I will miss you.

I gave Jakob a Sandman ban for the first time for two days. He was truly angry and sad and cried. I dried his tears and cleaned his nose and explained that two days would soon be over.

He must not hurt me or anyone else.

His ear-pulling was painful, also dangerous. Jakob must know his limits.

I realise how dependent our children are on television: Sandman, Sesame Street, Willi wants to

know, Dandelion, Little Amadeus, Pippi Longstocking, Jim Button, Lucky Luke, Vicky ...
and in no time the list is full of programs for a small child. But it was unbelievable that my son was already watching TV for half an hour a day. This is too much. I will give him the choice of choosing a single broadcast for fifteen minutes.

1-Euro-Job

I got a request from the Job Centre to take a so-called one-Euro job. For this they have commissioned an office in Berlin-Mitte. It is a company located on a factory floor in Hackescher Markt. They look competent. They give me a 1-Euro job at a health centre in Zehlendorf. I introduce myself and then realise they are looking for a cleaning lady. I am qualified as a hotel specialist, insurance specialist, sales manager and have over twenty years of professional experience. I am overqualified. Qualified enough to clean toilets, eight toilets a day.

Overqualified? Herniated discs? Nobody cares about all that, so long as you are employed. That you also must do your household chores, and everything for your child, all yourself, is all your problem. It was your decision to want a child. You could have continued to climb your career ladder: business trips, business lunches, good conversations, interesting people, further education. You wanted the child, didn't you?
Nobody is interested in the fact that you previously paid taxes for around twenty years. The tax office wants five thousand Euros from you for last year, and the loan, which wasn't one, is still outstanding. You must sign an oath of disclosure.
Then you will be left alone. You get a new identity, so to speak. Your old one is gone forever.

You have to disclose your bank accounts and everything you own, to show that you have nothing. You can only get a new bank account without any overdraft facility, only a credit account.

What choice do you have?

None.

I go on. Clean my eight toilets every day and over two hundred square meters in six hours. This includes two thousand square meters of garden.

Suddenly, the executive floor also needs support. I write advertising texts, design mailings and flyers, advertisements, and business letters. One to two hours a day.

I have to spend the rest of the time with vacuum cleaner and rubber gloves.

The colleagues are nice. The cook too. Jaques comes from the Caribbean, a tall Frenchman with a charming accent. I get a cough. Ignore it until it gets so bad that I can't talk anymore. Have the feeling that I have to throw up.

I have one week of training in the job centre office in Mitte. The hopelessness of the German labour market is discussed in a demanding but open manner.

Propaganda is being put out for people to look for work in other countries or to become self-employed. Thank you very much, I have already tried both.

I am on sick leave, unfortunately longer than fourteen days, which means that I automatically drop out of the 1-Euro job.

The bank takes the last additional 158 € earned on the following reason:
"It is not recognisable that these are social benefits!"

When I can no longer sleep through, I accept the kind offer of a little holiday to the Baltic Sea from my parents. Before they arrive on a farm in Grossenbrode, we could stay some days with a friend of theirs in Süssau. Mrs. Sehfeld is an elderly widow who lives together with her spoilt, tiny dog in a big house close to the beach. Before we pack, we celebrate my Fortieth birthday.
Jaques is surprisingly also coming to my birthday, just arriving, after all my other guests were gone.
He brings flowers and a homemade pizza.
Our first kiss opens a door.
My heart is dancing.
I'm in love!

Sea breeze

Finally, after all those hours travelling, the bus stopped in every single little village, I'm lying in my bed. It's well over twenty degrees, sweating. Jakob sleeps on the floor next to me on a mattress, like a stone. We live in Mrs. Sehfeld's house in the guest room. I can call her Ingrid.

The bus ride was exhausting, seven hours. Jakob was very brave, didn't even whinge. He sleeps very deeply with glowing red cheeks. Two hours by the sea in this wonderful air was good for him. He was happy that he could bring his scooter from home. The whole trip and last night I thought about Jacques. Mon amour, never out of my mind.

Jakob says Grandma Ilse, my mum, is the best Grandma for him. "Yes, she's not the best mum for you, but she is the best Grandma for me!"

I finally understand what it is all about. I've noticed that I need more rest.
Silence.
Being by myself feels good.
At night, finally I'm alone.

Do I want to blame Jakob for all of this? It's like I'm just doing my duty, taking care of him. What's wrong with me and my child, I don't feel like a mother should.

Why?

Because I don't want to know how he really is? Why don't I want to know how he really is? Because then I would understand how bad Jakob really feels. Why is he not feeling well?

Because I can't love you?

Why can't I love you?

Because I can't tell you, that your father didn't want us to have a baby?

Because I feel guilty, that I still wanted to give birth to you and want you to be with me?

Because I give you all the blame, for my work situation, for my financial situation, the many debts?

In God's name, my child is not guilty for anything!

The Baltic Sea was stormy today. We went swimming anyway. Jakob with orange water wings and a bright blue rubber ring. I bought him a little red boat today. He is doing so well. He misses his friends. Have sent twelve postcards today, reporting about the daily lemon ice cream.

"Mum, remember just think of the next broom stroke, then finally all the road is clean!"
Momo is his favorite book.
"Mum, you really are a very nice mum. All children should have a mum like you. It's really nice to live with you. I could live with you all my life. "
That feels so good. My child, you mean the world to me.

Tomorrow mum&dad will finally arrive. We're happy! I bought a bottle of rosé wine, some nuts and a few apples, which we will place in their room to welcome them.
We will also pick a bouquet in the meadows.

The day is muggy. Breathe deeply for my bronchitis. It was raining, including thunder and lightning.
Jakob was in the garden, ran naked in the rain and cheered for joy. I have not seen him so relaxed for a long time.
Mum&dad should have, by now, arrived in Grossenbrode.

I understood that I wanted my child so much and that the father was just the gardener.

The German Shepherd barks. It is early in the morning. The cows can already be heard. A few flies circle me. Jakob is still sleeping.

Yesterday we were with mum&dad in Travemünde, had a really nice day: sunshine and warm wind, harbour atmosphere of a small marina. There were baked potatoes with sour cream and smoked salmon, ice cream and cappuccino. Luxury!

Jakob and dad found a message in an old Sinalco bottle and sent it on its way again, with a new message.

I really enjoyed these wonderful, creative ideas with mum&dad as a child.

They are a special couple.

Taking a vacation means looking at a different way of life.

Deep thoughts

I read. Süddeutsche Zeitung / Jorge Semprun:
"What a beautiful Sunday. The Russian prisoners also fled Buchenwald in spring. In fact, they did not even flee, they evaporated. They suddenly stopped handling the spade or the hoe. They sat up. Perhaps a mild wind, smelling of all the juices of spring, had rustled the nearby leaves. Maybe you could hear birds chirping. In Buchenwald, at least surrounded by the dark and proud mass of a lush beech forest, you never heard birds singing. You never saw birds.
There were no birds on the Ettersberg.
Perhaps the birds could not stand the stench of burned flesh that spewed across the landscape from the crematorium in thick clouds of smoke. Maybe they couldn't stand the barking of the wolfhounds of the SS guards."

I can hardly bear this topic.
Get stomach pressure right away.
How can it be possible that this was once reality in "our country"?
How is it possible that the people who have witnessed it themselves do not talk about it? Can they exclude the "accomplished" genocide from their consciousness?

Where do I live? Who am I with?

It is wonderful with Jaques. But yet there is something that does not make my heart happy.
I have a feeling that Jacques still has no place in his heart. He still speaks of Anna as "his wife".
She is still alive for him. I would like to know if I have a chance, but I don't want to ruin anything.

I actually wanted to talk to Jacques about us today. He had brought a good Bordeaux with him, that we enjoyed. Full-bodied, gentle, and profound, like his kiss. We loved each other and then looked at photo albums. Gosh, my wrinkles will hopefully go away soon. I still mentioned our relationship, he couldn't say anything.
Nothing at all. Our kiss lasted for an hour and then he left. And I just wanted to know what he was feeling.
Whose reality am I living?
I want to face my life.
The firs are silent, big, and dark and wet. Jakob paints: Bob the builder.

I want you to live! I want you to live, Jakob Meyer. My child.
That was the gulf which was always between us.
My therapist searched for it for weeks, we searched together and could not find it. Now it is out.
I WANT YOU TO LIVE!!!
I can't pull myself together again, I'm so thankful that it's finally out, sobbing like a child.
The secret, the forbidden, the immoral, the inhuman, the loveless, the rejected, the unwanted

child of your father. I made that decision on my own and it has haunted me to this day. I have no peace, no true love, although I wanted and want you so much and at all costs. I did everything I could to make you happy child, fighting like a lioness. I have been wounded many times. The knot has now burst asunder. I can finally take a deep breath. I'm so thankful that you exist.

My decision was right. Now it's good.

I once read the following sentence on Lanzarote:

"If you want to get ahead, first you have to turn around."

Today, for the first time in a long time, we didn't speak or see each other.

Jaques, I miss you.

The bad mood comes because of my menstruation. Read that women who have their menstruation can be more aggressive than usual.

Look over the insolvency documents. I created folders. It goes on. I don't want to be the victim of my circumstances; I want to earn money. Listen to "modern music" on classic radio.

Bye Bye

Roberta moves to Kiel in November. She already has an apartment and seems to have thought it over carefully.
I'm surprised. We will miss her a lot.

Jakob and Roberta are at *Pole Poppenspäler*, just the thing for them.
Enjoy the last late summer sun in the garden. Mrs. Landlord baked fresh plum cake. In front of the house police are there, because of a dispute in the neighboring house. Didn't even realised that one of them had drank himself to death. You can hardly believe how many alcoholics there are. Even the rich as well.

I already miss Roberta; I can't even think how it will be when she lives in Holstein permanently. Hopefully, she will be fine.
Jakob will also miss her, the afternoon hours in the "fairytale forest" and on the "beach", where she always sat on the stone, while Jakob was fishing. She taught Jakob so much. Songs. Poems. Flowers, trees and bird species. Although she was often strict and with an iron discipline, she was also loving. And funny too.
I have to let go.
Somehow you believe that it goes on like this forever. Only when something is no longer there, does it become clear what you had. I often say

goodbye to a person and am not aware that I may
never see them again.
Comrades together.

Two types only

I have a throbbing skull. Spent fifteen hours at my desk today. Insolvency appointment is tomorrow. Want to free myself from everything.
In Germany there is public discussion about the poverty in our society. I understand that I am not alone with my fate. Actually, there are only two types of people left: either you made it or you just don't belong anymore. Even if I wear clothes from the past, you can see my downfall. From now on you belong to the proletariat, to the "working class". If only there was work! Maybe there is still some work, but fewer and fewer people have to manage, despite more pressure. Or maybe not, then sooner or later they will come on board. Moin Moin!

I think hardly anyone understands me. The unemployment benefit has been paid to me for two years. Enough is enough. My skills are wasting away. I finally want to be challenged. I want to be integrated, recognised, accepted!

It will start in eight days. Mother and Child retreat. We look forward to Fehmarn.

Tomorrow morning at six they film in the street. Everyone has to park their cars around the corner. I would love to participate. In front of the camera, have fun, earn money and entertain. A dream.

Healing time

We are sitting in the direction of travel. The weather has cooled down a bit, which is normal for November. A snowstorm greets us, we are there.

My reflection is alien to me. Where is my beauty? Is it on vacation from me right now? Can I stay with me somehow? That seems to be a central question in my life.
Since the day we arrived, I've been wearing Grandma's passion killers and find it normal. Am I still sane?
I stuff myself blindly. Fear of loss. My resolution to do Qi Gong morning ritual has vanished, as if I had never done it. I watch myself and Jakob. Try to stop time so that we can start a new life.
My perm and the self-cut fringe don't look that good at the moment either. Jaques would say, if I am not satisfied with what I have now, how can I ever be?
Maybe he's right.

I enjoy spending time with Jakob on Fehmarn. We did a snowball fight yesterday. Today a long hike to the dike under a clear blue sky, along a stream, past sheep, horses and piled up turnips. Breathe soft sea air.

We spent three hours in Burg, the nearest town. The minibus took us along, with two other mothers and their children. We were shopping. I had twenty-three Euros with me. I was only able to get fifteen more from the cash machine. I felt sorry for Jakob. He wanted so much to have a compass. It was supposed to cost twenty-four Euros. Unfortunately, that exceeded my budget. And he couldn't help but cry and cry so bitterly that you could hear him all over the shop:

"Why do you always have no money, always no money? Others can buy things, but you always can't!"

Rent, electricity, telephone and kindergarden are paid for. The bills for the car insurance, the tuition fee and a last installment for clothes are still unpaid. They will probably all remind me again and add fees for it. Have been a bit more relaxed since I have placed everything in the hands of my insolvency adviser.

As a consolation we were in a café. There was blueberry pancake with cream and vanilla ice.

A soft wind blows from the sea.

The trees rustle.

Why do I only recognise each other's situation so often and am blind and trapped in my own? Fuck it, Hartz IV. I want to be accepted in society; I need recognition like everyone else. I had paid taxes for twenty years of my life before I got into this situation. I am allowed to make mistakes in life. Live to learn, not to be perfect.

I am allowed to forgive myself. Despite my anger. The most important thing is love. To love means to take the time to listen carefully. Looking you in the eye, stroking your hair, sitting on your bed, even when you're asleep. Appreciating you by my side. There is no second chance for the time we have together. Soon it will be over forever.

Maybe our children are born to show us the way which we have lost at some point?

Today we were at the sea. We drove with Corinna's VW bus, four women and five children, it was great fun. The lighthouse seemed huge to us. Unfortunately, the door was closed. Winter break. We hiked along the sea, four kilometres in strong winds. A great achievement especially for the children. The sea breeze has blown away my cold. With red cheeks we returned home for supper.

Jakob goes to play *Harry Potter* with Viktor. They get along well, although Viktor is often not that easy as an autistic boy.

His sister is a bit younger but is in no way inferior to him. Trixi is like a flea.

With Viktor's mum, I get on so well. Corinna works for an insurance company in Schwabia. She loves horses as much as I do.

A real buddy. Hope we can keep in touch.

This time we were seven altogether in the wave pool on the south beach. We understand each other perfectly, even the children get along well. Swap biscuits for candy, and swap other things.

"Here is my bodyboard!"

"Then you take my tyre for a while!"

We all have found each other. In the shop's special offer there were winter boots for 9.90 €, I bought them. Ten years ago, I would easily have spent twenty times as much for them in the *KaDeWe*. I used to buy almost everything there, even a chandelier.

Thanks mum

We are home again. The cure did us good.

With Jaques, the physical attraction is still there, but what else can I expect?

The midnight bells ring out. Called Roberta. She has arrived safely in her new home. We will miss her, not only on Monday evenings. I visited my family doctor today. She needed to discuss the results of the treatment with me. In the course report there are some positive things. But what struck me was a subordinate clause at the end: "Psychotherapeutic treatment is still advisable to clarify the causes that led to social and financial decline."
The decline was so obviously pronounced in my ears.

I was with mum in Dahlem for the medieval Christmas market. It was so nice. With cinnamon stars, mulled wine, and waffles with icing sugar.
Meanwhile Jakob was in the aquarium with his grandfather. There were even crocodiles there. Then directly opposite the Christmas market, at the Berlin memorial church. Dad had bought him pink candy floss twice. I always loved going to the *Third World Shop* next to the memorial church.
It was nice mum.
Thanks.

Holy Halls

I finally found the strength to send an unsolicited job application, where I did my apprenticeship: The Bristol Hotel Kempinski Berlin.

I have the telephone number of the personnel office in front of me. After almost an hour of hesitation, I overcome myself.

"Mr. Rosenthal, please!"

"Do you have an appointment?"

"No, I would like to make an appointment with Mr. Rosenthal."

"He is busy today, but what is it about?"

The friendly assistant recommended that I hand in my documents the same afternoon. I should have her called through the front desk. On the way there, I still looked good. Styled to the tips of my hair, I felt like a winner.

The feeling of walking again in the "Holy Halls" of Kempi was familiar, although twenty years had passed. The carpets, the bare floor, flower arrangements, the barely audible whir of the air conditioning, female assistants in red uniforms. A prominent pop singer entered by the main door, in a red tartan laissez-faire look, which suits her. The assistant came, beamed at me, I returned her smile. Handshake. That afternoon I felt so good. Happiness hormones. I had a delicate gloss applied to my lips, my hair pinned up, dark costume and my blue cashmere coat. I talked about the good old days, the nice colleagues from way back then, and those who had moved to Australia and California and so on.

But I don´t say a word about Norbert, who was working here as a bartender at the time. He was finally sacked because of his strange belt buckle, which he provocatively kept wearing, and who was now the father of Jakob.

I made myself clear, that I had a non-hotel industry career but that I was now asking for another chance. She was impressed.

"You'll hear from us this week!"

Today is Friday.

Nevertheless, the encounter in the top-class hotel was good for me.

I feel healed.

From what, I am not so sure.

Maybe I thought that my apprenticeship at this hotel was just a dream.

Reality finally caught up with me.

Who feels sorry?

Full moon.
My most sensitive area hurts so much. The day before yesterday he took me from behind. I challenged Jacques and wanted a second round. He switched on his turbo and apparently something broke within me. Go to see my doctor tomorrow. He hasn't called me since.

I cried during today's therapy session, and the truth broke out of me right at the start.
With Jaques it is over.
Last Friday gave me the rest.
I should have said STOP.
It wasn't his intention to hurt me.
But my soul trembles all way to the bottom.
My inner child, I'm sorry.
I want to take better care of myself.

Everything that lies behind me is over and gone.
The maintenance advance from the youth welfare office is there. Three days before Christmas.
I am so happy that I cry.
Thanks.

Santa Claus lives

Granddad Willi's Christmas record is on. Got my laptop on, post code search. Christmas cards have to be sent out. It is quite dark in the afternoon. We are at the forest festival, invitation from *Globetrotter*. There was stick bread around the campfire.

Night hike at 5 pm in the afternoon.

The branches crack under our feet. You can no longer see anything. Jakob's hands are warm. In front of and behind us are dozens of children with their families. Nobody really knows where we go. And then the foremost see something and call, come quickly, come quickly!

Incredible.

In the middle of the forest, sitting there with a white, long beard, red coat, and red cap, the frozen Santa Claus, surrounded by bulging sacks!

He can speak properly and really sounds the way you always imagine him to be. You always think it is an invention, but he really does exist! We saw him in person.

We all had to cope with that at first.

When Santa Claus finally sat around the campfire with all of us, he finally unpacked his sacks. He distributed working flashlights and gingerbread cookies and Santa Clauses made of chocolate.

From then on, many lights sparkled through the evening. It was special.

Special days

The tree sparkles in the light. These are special days.
Covered beds, cleared corners, hand-crafted cards. The fridge keeps the secret of the cookies.
Carpets, curtains now want attention, as well as mirrors, windows, and doors.
ATMs run hot. Everything pulls on my wallet, if I only had one…
Car park places fought over. It is bustling in supermarkets.
Wish lists fill up, people whisper. Paper and ribbons rustle, afternoon nap is postponed.
Ironing, wood polish, computer on standby.
Granddad's LP, I sing along to it all day.
Christmas greetings flutter into the house.
The children chatter, sing songs, we hug, tell each other truths of the heart. Christmas is over.

It was a special time.
My life has me back again.

Hope

I had a job interview with the insurance company. They want to take me on board, because I have all the qualifications I need, in order to work as an agent! I just have to adapt my knowledge to the current state of the market. It should start in mid-January with a company car and a fixed salary! Can't believe it yet.

I thought it through. We need a babysitter for my evening appointments. Because I earn over 1500 € net, I can pay the babysitter. That should be possible.

I'm so happy.

Grit called me from Lanzarote, asked when I want to pick up my bags? She is right. Almost two years have passed. Oh my god, what have I been doing since then?

I called Marianne and asked if we could live with her in the finca. She agreed and is looking forward to seeing us. Grandma gave me the money for our last-minute tickets. I want to pay it back to her gradually. I will soon be earning real money! Will take spaghetti packs with us and hope that it will still be nice.

Our alarm clock will go off at 4.30 am tomorrow. We fly to Lanzarote.

Arrived again

The sea glistens in the moonlight. The kitchen curtain moves in a delicate breeze. Jakob still calls, he wants to have a drink and hold my hand. The same habits every night, no matter where we are.

How this full moon is reflected in the sea, it looks like it could last forever. It has always been, and always will be.

We arrived the day before yesterday. We feel good staying with Marianne and Scott. I contacted Katharina and Grit I'll meet them before the weekend. Yesterday's trip to the mountains, as Jakob calls them, was familiar and full of memories.

For me Lanzarote is still home, a different one though.

The day was beautiful. Marianne took us to a magical area. First, we went with the Corsa, an old path, like a serpentine into the mountains. We parked the car in a ditch on the edge of a Campo, onto which a dry riverbed opened. 17 ° C, clouds and wind escort us.

We are between Haria and Marguez.

First it is easy, then steeper uphill, past magical rare flowers. The smallest fingernail seems larger than the tiny goblets of colour, in violet, pink, yellow and white. Fennel blossom are reminiscent of sweets. Stones inhabited by lichens, in orange and lime green. Giant cacti, grasses as tall as ferns. Thorn bushes weave in and out, with their tiny flowers in pink and white, undergrowth, old palm trees.

Stones. Rock. Dust. Alternating sun, wind, and clouds. Always changing. Layers on, layers off, like an onion. Hat on, hat off and on and off again. Jakob and Scott also alternate constantly with the position of the scout. Strangely, the riverbed runs ever wider upwards until we come to a small pine grove. Halfway, we treated ourselves to a picnic to fortify ourselves, consisting of apple, crispbread, and water, on a carpet of long pine needles.

The view down into the vastness of the valley, to the deep blue coast with its foaming waves, many kilometers away, repays our efforts.

The children play in tree hollows.

The descent is pleasant, my collector's heart is delighted with a bouquet of flowers for our apartment. Back in the car, relief, sit. A look in the mirror. Blurred mascara, messy hair, happiness in the eye.

The candle flickers in its own gold. The Canary Islands are shown on the label of the wine bottle. Lanzarote is special. But how can I say that? I never really got to know the other six islands. I could have done that in the past eleven years. It was probably because of fear of disloyalty. You took me in like a mother, let me feel life, challenged my values, chewed me up and spat me out. Caressing me lovingly and healing my wounds. Both a carrot and a stick. Last time it was too much.

I almost died. Only this time I also had the care and responsibility for my child. I have to close the window, I'm cold. My first glass of red wine was delicious. Now this moonlit night begins with the second and a just opened bag of Frutas secas.

At the airport, Katharina says goodbye to me like only a friend can do. She brings me lava stones and black sand, shells and a candle that can swim on the water. So that I never forget the island. Then she pulls out a bag from under the table, full of branches from her cactus collection. I love her like a sister. Take care of yourself.

We are back in Wannsee. Glad to be in my bed. The trip was a milestone.
Can finally let go.
I am free.
Looking forward to the new job, the new life.

Burn for life

The work has been exhausting. We had training in the morning. Customer service in the evening. Everything is still a bit unusual.
Some customers treat me like most sales agents are treated. It hurts a little. Must learn to deal with it more pragmatically. Fortunately, I have time for Jakob in the morning and in the afternoon. The babysitter comes from 7:00 pm to 9:30 pm. It works quite well. Jakob is also enthusiastic about her. She is there for him and he gets all her attention.
Fortunately, tomorrow is the weekend. The colleagues who have no children, have work to work then.

I can try out life models if I am willing to accept the consequences. That is my experience. Isn't life made for looking at life models, trying them out and experiencing how flexible people really are?
The responsibility is mine, no one else's. Burn for life, not just for enduring.

The first. It's hard to believe.
I finally have more money in my account than in the past three years.
The dry spell was long.
Certainly, there are people who have had to make do with less for a lot longer.
I now know what it means to live frugally.
Humility.

I am so thankful that things are going uphill. I am going to buy a pair of pants for Jakob today, and a new pair of shoes for me.

There is still something in me that does not give peace yet.
My heart is pounding.
It's longing, longing for real love.
I need the right man.
Jakob lacks a dad that he can rely on.

Snow. Tomorrow at ten I will meet Edgar Schrotz in the café. He asked for an appointment.

Are we not quits? Forgiveness is necessary. I do not want him to have any hopes. He should finally leave me alone. My soul really suffered, so did Jakob´s.
What happens to the financial debt? I don't trust this peace. Will see what my insolvency advisor recommends. I can still rely on her.

What is important? Music? Love? Time? God? Leave me alone. No - don't leave me alone. I need suport, I want to do my job as a woman, as a life partner. I finally want a husband.

I had the struggle of my life on Lanzarote. I was worried, didn't know how to get groceries anymore.

It was terrible. If you wanted ice cream, I couldn't buy you one. I could rarely fulfill a wish for you. This time shook me. This time took away my pride and primal trust. This had carried me invincibly through time. Arduous, very arduous, I have to work through every step to myself anew. I don't want to lose love and belief that we can live a good life on our own. I have taken the first steps; I am no longer dependent on the job center.

Tomorrow I have my penultimate therapy session. Spring is here. Cherry blossoms awaken. Hyacinths exude their fragrance. I always remember the first mown grass.

There was money today! Jakob could buy his longed for "Micky Mouse" book. He kissed me in the shop.

Sparks in life

I'm finally starting to feel my child. As if I saw him for the first time. My boy, how are you? Perhaps I have failed to give you all the years what you urgently needed? A father?
End of therapy. I feel numb, torn apart, and yet clear. Act on my own responsibility. I want to find a middle way, a feasible way. Not everything is resolved by force, I should learn to be patient and remain authentic. Is that possible?

I spoke to Grandma Klara about the sparks in life that only spark rarely.

Have read the Fengshui book, our apartment urgently needs to clear out.

I meet an old colleague of Vitessa at the recycling center. If I remember well, she owns a sophisticated dating agency, she has for many years.
"Call me, I'm in every phone book!"
I no longer believe in coincidences. After a few days, I find her.

"Oh, I don't do this any longer. We couldn't keep up with the online companies. If you want to find a partner in a serious way, I recommend a company that is scientifically sound and internationally networked. Parship!"

Am I ready for it?

I logged in for six months.

I have to apply for a stipendium from the Berlin Senate Office. Maybe I'm lucky and the right person reads my texts.

The new job is fun. Finally, I have a permanent position. My first successes give me a boost. When I come home from a customer, Jakob is already sleeping. Then I sit down a bit at the desk. It's going forwards.

On the recommended online dating service, there is actually someone who interests me more closely. We have been sending mails to each other for three weeks. Only one a day, how exciting! Already looking forward to his answers.
It's almost unbearable!
Each of his mails closes with the words:
"Take good care of yourself and your child!"
It sounds true as rarely anyone says that.

New Year's Eve I swore to myself:
"This is my year!"
Maybe it's true.

The gentleman writes to me every day during his lunch break. Butterflies flutter. I think I fell in love.

I submitted twenty pages of my first manuscript to the Berlin Senate Office. Hope my scholarship will be approved.

I hang up the phone and stay silent.
I hardly dare to breathe.
Suddenly everything is so calm.
After six weeks of correspondence, we have just spoken for the first time.

What was that? Am I crazy? He's coming to Berlin!
He comes to visit me!
Feel like a teenager.
I don't even know your surname, nor your phone number or neither your address.

Is every May like a new life?

The sun is shining.
Listening to Mozart.
The best start for today.
He comes!
Arrival at 2:30 pm Tegel Airport.

"Once you have found yourself, you cannot lose anything in this world anymore!"

Stefan Zweig

Thanks

…where to start with so many good spirits …
Thanks to my son, for your love, your clarity, and for
believing in me.
Thanks to my husband, you carry me through all times
with your love. With you I can stay authentic.
Thanks to my parents, your openness to the world, and
for always believing in a happy ending.
Thanks to my great grandma, I miss you so much!
Thanks to my brothers who forgave me for my
adventures into life.
Thanks to friends who are and have been by my side,
here in particular:
Beta-Renate, Verena, Michaela and Tanja.

I also need to thank my first publisher,
Mr. Siegfried Heinrichs, from Oberbaum Verlag, who
has unfortunately passed away. Without you, today I
would still write to myself, in my quiet little room.
You discovered something in my way of writing and
were a good teacher to me. And thanks to Mr.
Heinrich's wife, Marina, who is to `blame` for
everything anyway. Thanks also to the support team of
BoD, here I feel to be in good hands, I am professionally
looked after, safe plenty of money and yet are free.
I should have tried this years ago and not hesitated for
so long, what a waist of time…
Thank you my friends, all over the world,
for accepting me how I am.

Martina

P.S. Oh yeah…and great Thanks to my
guardian angel, I am sorry, that
I always keep you so very busy xxx

Dear reader, don't worry, Martina C. Bund
(the C. stands for Christiane, I was baptised like
this), and Martina Hammond, both names are
only me, one and the same person.
My maiden name was Bund, when I was born,
1966 in Berlin.
When I finally got married 2009 in England, I was
happy to take my husband's name on board.

In case you would like to give me your feedback
on this book, I am already looking forward to
reading your lines.

Please don't take it personally if I do not answer,
but I try my best.

we-call-this-living@web.de

Your thoughts and words will for sure mean a lot
to me.

Also it would make me happy, if you like to talk
about this book to other people.

May you always be blessed, Carpe Diem!

Martina

"Didn't put the book down and read through it in an afternoon. Like a thunderstorm of flashlights, the author illuminates a phase of her life that would have driven many other people to the brink. She lets the reader participate with concise sentences, sometimes profoundly brilliant, sometimes everyday direct. Alternating between oppressive, harrowing and joyful, grateful descriptions, it guides the reader through the stages of life she has experienced intensely.

Martina Bund encourages you to never give up hope, to believe in life and in love. This is the proof, that models of life can not only be thought, but also lived."

Claudine Krause, 2016 at Amazon